A Nosegay
of Pleasant Delights

Available from Evertype

By Brian S. Lee

Prince Conrad: A Fairy Tale (2016)

The Aventures of Alys in Wondyr Lond
(Lewis Carroll's *Alice* in Middle English, 2013)

Other short story collections

Nosy Neighbours: Stories in Mennonite Low German and English
Nieschieaje Nohbasch: Jeschichte opp Plautdietsch enn Enjlisch
(Jack Thiessen 2015)

Neighbours: Stories in Mennonite Low German and English
Nohbasch: Jeschichte opp Plautdietsch enn Enjlisch
(Jack Thiessen 2014)

The Partisan and other Stories (Gabriel Rosenstock,
tr. Mícheál Ó hAodha & Gabriel Rosenstock 2014)

The Book of Poison (Panu Petteri Höglund & S. Albert Kivinen,
tr. Colin Parmer & Tino Warinowski 2014)

The Burning Woman and other stories (Frank Roger 2012)

A Nosegay
of Pleasant Delights

Five-minute fictions
by
Brian S. Lee

Illustrated by
Laura Anne Passarello

evertype
2016

Published by Evertype, 73 Woodgrove, Portlaoise, R32 ENP6, Ireland.
www.evertype.com.

Text © 2016 Brian S. Lee.
Illustrations © 2016 Laura Anne Passarello.

First edition 2016.

A catalogue record for this book is available from the British Library.

ISBN-10 1-78201-146-3
ISBN-13 978-1-78201-146-0

Set in Minion Pro and Étienne by Michael Everson.

Cover: Michael Everson.
Cover photograph by Ukrainian photographer "Es75", dreamstime.com.

Printed by: LightningSource.

Contents

A Nosegay
of Pleasant Delights

1

A Space Odyssey

Coursing rapidly towards the planet Invisum, a compacted mass of unknown composition that was circling or rather ellipsing the star Proculabest in the galaxy Ophthen, Blogdonnik gazed intently at the console in his lap. Reproduction on Domum being asexual, the word "his" to refer to him must do neutral duty as the default adjective in the absence of a genderless one in English. The readings on the console on which he depended for a safe landing on Invisum were changing too fast for his virtual intelligence to absorb, beamed to him as it was from an ever more swiftly receding Domum. At the rate of attraction exerted by Ophthen on his passage through inter-galactic space, he would have needed a

heart larger than his chest to keep a brain irrigated, and a head the size of a carbuncle; consequently he had no brain to speak of, or from. Instead the ideas, thoughts, knowledge, hopes and intentions that he had acquired during his Domum-years of residence there, aimed along his pre-arranged path, followed his trajectory, and kept up with him by innate re-infusions of kinetic energy. The farther he went the greater the effort required to keep tabs on the mental stragglers that tended to lag behind, and the less attention he could consequently spare for the data windowing more and more speedily across his screen.

But now among the stars of Ophthen at last, he watched as the pre-aligned coordinates locked securely on to their still invisible destination. On Domum the machine had been made fail-safe. Once programmed it could act in only one way: the right way. But suddenly it spoke its first dire warning. That is, it interrupted the non-molecular stream of consciousness emanating from Domum to inform the luckless Blogdonnik "You are too close!" Before he had time to learn what this meant in physical terms, he was again interrupted by the more urgent "You are TOO close!" And hastily on the heels of that message came the fateful "You are MUCH too close!"

The data that the console was dutifully relaying to Domum, when deciphered by the intelligences there, revealed that a miscalculated magnetic storm of quarks, ions and small body parts emitted from the outsize star Proculabest, once dubbed Satisprocul by gloomy opponents of Blogdonnik's venture, but a misnomer now, had interfered with the soft-landing settings on the console that should have deposited Blogdonnik safely on the surface of Invisum, whatever the consistency of that surface should prove to be. Reprogrammed in effect, the machine was thrusting Blogdonnik and his protective capsule inexorably towards total disintegration on the planet he had been intending to colonize, if environmentally suitable, by self-induced cell division. Frantically relayed from distant Domum came the urgent orders AVOID, and then AVERT, and finally and vainly ABORT.

The implosion, at near-maximum velocity, momentarily lit up the darkness of deep space, as columns of iridescent material thousands of miles long spewed upwards from the impacted surface, before freezing and falling lightlessly back. The flash was detected on Domum, where it looked like the dancing gleam of a candle-flame seen far off in a forest through a gap in leaves too briefly blown aside, taunting the wanderer with an illusory hope of shelter. Blogdonnik, space ship and contents were instantly vapourized, not liquefying-time allowed, and distributed into sub-atomic particles which ploughed their way forcibly through the interstices of the planet's molecular composition, but were gradually slowed down as the intense pressure of opposing components reduced their progress almost to a standstill.

And eventually they were forced together, re-combined and fused into fantastical fresh configurations of unguessed complexity, which were in turn kneaded and moulded into a new whole. Then out at the other side of Invisum exuded a Shethecon, a new and violently newborn species of supra-human activity, that was swept away by the repulsive magnetic pole of Abiprocul.

But not helplessly. Gathering herself together with vigour and determination, shipless but not shapeless she set course for home. Absorbing in her progress the now elongated transmission from Domum, and amalgamating within herself the squeezed components of the console, from which the intelligence she was receiving enabled her to extract, interpret and reappraise the data it had mindlessly gathered, the Shethecon began her return journey to change forever the orientation of the inhuman inhabitants of Blogdonnik's Domum.

2

Snedronningen

OK, so I admit I took the tour because Kyle was going on it. That's not entirely true, though, for in fact I took it because Isabel insisted on going as well. Or rather, Kyle insisted on taking her. It puzzled me then to know what he could see in her, but understanding him better now I realize it was everything blatantly false, superficial and repellent—her supposedly good looks, admirable in a town where there wasn't much competition, her brains, just enough to get her admitted to the second-rate college where Kyle had a football scholarship on the strength of his splendid physique, and her supercilious habit of looking down her nose at everything,

except when she was fluttering her eyelashes up at him. Kyle and I had been playmates since our first schooldays, until he met this Isabel while I was working to save up for I don't know what, perhaps this make-or-break tour.

"Rather go to Italy, Gerda," my mother said. "There's the leaning tower, and Michelangelo's statues, and Roman ruins, and gondolas, and Blue grottoes. In Denmark there's just a metal mermaid on a rock, and she's quite disappointingly small, they say."

"That's where the tour's going," I answered firmly.

"Well, I'm glad you know some of the people on it. Kyle's a nice boy, and a clever girl like that pretty Isabel can be a good friend to you."

"Sure," I grunted sarcastically.

We landed in wonderful Copenhagen, and the guide took us to a cheap hotel (comparatively speaking) close to the Tivoli gardens, where naturally Kyle wanted to treat Isabel to some of the exciting rides. They cost extra, so I preferred to walk up past the Amalienborg palace to see the Little Mermaid; OK she *was* small, and you couldn't get near her for tourists trying to clamber round her rock; and then back via another palace in a lush park full of topless women sunning themselves on the grass.

"Just as well Kyle's not here," I thought. "Some of them aren't fit to be seen, but some, I freely admit, would have made his heart stop."

It was an awfully long way, and I was worn out by the time I got back to the hotel.

"We've had a wonderful time," gushed Isabel, "although I was absolutely *terrified* on that roller coaster thing, wasn't I, Kyle? What a pity, Gerda, you missed our bus ride to the Little Mermaid, and I won't even say what we saw in the parks, and—"

If we'd been alone, I'd have blacked the eyes under those dreadful lashes, I would indeed.

At Roskilde, the original capital, we saw the exhumed remains of Viking ships. "Not very seaworthy," Isabel remarked scornfully.

"Wouldn't you row out with me in one of them?" Kyle laughed. She sniffed.

"*I* would, all the way to Bornholm and back, if only you'd ask me," I said bitterly to myself.

"I wanted to go to Helsingør, where Hamlet killed Claudius," Isabel complained. "That's Elsinore, you know," she added for my benefit, since I hadn't been to college, "but it's in the wrong direction!"

In Odense we crowded into the little street where Hans Andersen had been born. We couldn't all go indoors—there were too many of us—but it was thrilling to be there, or would have been, if Isabel hadn't snorted and said "Fancy *living* in a place like this! No wonder Dickens couldn't get rid of him when he visited his mansion on Gad's Hill!"

"Did he?" I asked doubtfully.

"*We* know he did, don't we, Kyle?" Isabel appealed to him archly.

Why did he smile back at her, unless his eye was blinded and his heart cicatrized by a sliver of the Snow Queen's deadening mirror?

Aarhus meant a bit of a detour, for which we'd paid extra. The scenery was certainly beautiful, but Isabel grimaced at the miniature model village we were shown, and said how poky the rooms must be. What did she expect of houses two feet high?

In a field at Ribe we found a monument to Dagmar, Denmark's first Queen, on what we were told was the site of her castle. "Draughty in winter," Isabel growled; but she was already grumpy from walking in high-heeled shoes up medieval streets in the town.

No wonder she didn't want to climb the steps in the cathedral tower, but Kyle said it was a pity to come so far and not get the view from the top. I followed some way behind, rather irritably because they had gone on without even looking back to see where I was. It was tough going, I must say. And after sixty or so steps, there she was coming down, pushing past the ascending tourists with a grim frown on her disgruntled face.

"Where's Kyle?" I asked, hiding my delight behind a look of concern.

"Insisted on going on up, although I told him I'd had enough!"

"Men!" I said, my heart pounding, not just from the stairs.

"Go on if you want to, but it gets worse farther up."

Somehow I reached the top, with some other panting members of the party, all of 246 steps above blessed terra firma.

Kyle was taking pictures of the surrounding countryside. "Well done," he said, smiling at me. "Stand over there where I can photograph you, with the wind blowing through your hair." And into my lungs, perched on the balustrade, if he liked!

"Horrors, don't climb up there," he said. "Isabel's afraid of heights, and testy. I should have had *you* on those Tivoli rides!"

"Or sky diving or bungee jumping," I laughed recklessly, tossing the hair he'd wanted to photograph.

"Too risky," he frowned, to my relief. "These top steps may be dangerous, going down. Shall I hold your arm?"

"And my hand, and my singing heart," I told myself, clutching his muscular arm with just the right amount of assumed nervousness, and no intention of ever letting go.

3

Free Dinner

"If we win on Saturday," the Master announced, "there will be free dinner on Sunday for the whole college."

"Isn't that a little impetuous, Master," remonstrated the Bursar, "considering our budget?"

"We'd have to subtract less from their caution money," the Master admitted, "but the other team hasn't lost a final in six years (I've been meaning to complain about that college's habit of scooping all the best athletes) and in any case it's only the men in digs without prior engagements whom the kitchen staff may have to cater extra for. If necessary tell them to scrap

the fish course and give everybody one less roast potato— except at the high table, of course."

The Junior Common Room President enthusiastically set about organizing the college fan club. He hired a donkey cart, decorated it with flags and bunting, and sporting a monocle and top hat paraded with his committee down the High, the team's vociferous supporters marching to drums and trumpets behind them. Policemen walked in front, serene and official, with a sergeant and outsize new recruit at the back, to see that nobody on the way to the playing field upset the public or obstructed the traffic roaring past in the street.

"Are we expecting trouble?" the recruit asked.

"Always," the sergeant drily answered.

"What are our chances of winning the supper?" a hungry committee member asked.

"Zero," said the President. "They've three internationals, including the England captain."

"He's not supposed to be playing. He's got to be available for the Barbarians match next week."

"He's down as A. N. Other, but everyone there will know who he is. But maybe—" a speculative look came into the eye the monocle didn't obscure.

The marchers were about to pass under the windows of the rival college, where jeering team members and supporters were leaning out to mock them. The President hopped down from the cart to warn the leading policeman to stop the traffic as the procession was going to have to veer across to the right-hand side of the road, "in case they bomb us!"

"Bomb?" said the policeman in alarm, hurrying white-gloved into the middle of the street.

"Keep close to the pedestrians on the pavement," the President ordered the driver of the cart, "and swing across the road as soon as someone's hit. The police will stop the traffic."

"This donkey won't swing," grunted the driver. "He knows his own pace."

An elderly townsman, impeded by the donkey's nose pressing against his elbow, looked up just as the first paper package missed the President's top hat and burst in a soapy shower of dirty bathwater over the old man's head and shoulders.

"I saw who threw it, sir!" cried the President. He sprang again from the cart to summon sergeant and police recruit to comfort the irate and soaking-wet pedestrian, while traffic backed up behind the reluctant donkey and strolling marchers crossing the road.

"Schoolboy high spirits, sir," the sergeant said soothingly. "No harm intended."

"*Pub* spirits! I'm soaked!" exclaimed the man, jumping to avoid a second packet. "You've got to arrest every man jack of the hooligans!"

"This way!" cried the President, hurrying through the college gates and up the stairs to the rooms overlooking the street. The burly recruit followed, with the sergeant and bedraggled victim trailing behind him.

"Trespassing!" cried the bombers.

"Don't any of you read law?" demanded the President. "You committed a felony, and it's habeas corpus!"

"Habby's what?" said the burly recruit.

"Have his ass," explained an American student.

"The ass," said the President, waving majestically out of the window at the donkey cart on the other side of the street, "is innocent."

"Will you lay a charge, sir?" the sergeant asked, with his notebook out.

"Of dynamite, if I could," panted the wet pedestrian.

"Well, you can't," said the largest man in the room. "We've got to go and get ready for the match."

"It was him, sir, I mean he, who doused you!" exclaimed the President eagerly.

"Ready for the match? No harm intended? Ready *with* it, Guy Fawkes! You've lit it, and burnt your fingers," his steaming target expostulated.

"Like Latimer and Ridley in the Broad!" agreed the recruit, laying a heavy hand on the big man's shoulder.

"Do you know who I am?" the huge forward shouted, preparing to break through yet another tackle.

"Been on television, then, have you, sir?" sneered the sergeant, jingling handcuffs. "Now you'll be in the newspapers, too. Want to wear these, or come quietly as you are?"

The rival team and their supporters looked on in consternation as their best player was led away. "We'll catch the blighters at the field, and they'll wish they hadn't come," someone said threateningly. And helter-skelter they rushed out in pursuit of their opponents' procession, the unperturbed donkey now plodding sedately over Magdalen bridge.

* * *

"So what actually happened?" the deputy President asked. "Why was the dinner cancelled? We won the trophy, didn't we?"

"We were awarded it, we didn't win it," grunted the President gloomily. "The other college was more interested in causing a riot than in rugby, especially with the better half of their team under arrest, so the station commander ordered the police to bar entrance to the field, and the game had to be abandoned. We weren't the spoil sports who caused the disturbance, so we got the cup."

"Then why not the dinner?"

"I failed there," the President conceded bitterly. "Legal wrangling over the wording of the Master's proclamation. He

13

said 'If our team wins,' but they didn't play, so they didn't win, did they?"

"Seems like special pleading."

"Bursar was looking pretty smug. But," the President added, brightening, "we made headlines in all the newspapers: 'England captain arrested after college fracas.' He's been sacked, of course. Tough, but that's the price of fame, I suppose."

4

The Bag on the Bench

"If only we were rich, what a difference it would make!" I said wistfully.

"It would that," my wife agreed.

It was a fine day, so I left her to her kitchen chores and took my newspaper to my favourite bench in the park.

There was a stranger sitting there, in a greatcoat with the collar turned up round his ears. I wasn't to be denied, so I sat down on the empty half of the bench beside him. He was holding an old leather bag on the seat between us. He glanced furtively at me, but didn't say anything or move off as I opened my newspaper. After a few minutes I opened the

paper even wider, almost touching his shoulder with it, to show I wasn't intimidated. I think he shrank a little away, but only settled his ears deeper in his collar and remained silent. Soon he gave the bag a little pat, as if it had been a pet dog, and let his hand fall on to his knee.

For some time there was no sound but the wind in the trees and the occasional rustle of my newspaper.

Then I noticed a young woman, possibly his daughter, hesitantly approach. She seemed agitated, as she took his arm, with a frightened glance at me, and hauled him away, talking volubly in some nightmarish gibberish, which he apparently answered in the same unintelligible fashion. They were nearly at the park end before I realized that he had forgotten his bag. I snatched it up, and hurried after them. But he waved me urgently away, grinning and gesticulating with apologetic grunts of his uncouth language, plainly indicating I could do anything I liked with his bag, except give it back to him. Next moment they'd scampered across the road and around a corner where I had no intention of following.

A sudden horrifying thought struck me. Was the bag ticking? I dropped it and sprinted for the shelter of the trees. But there was no explosion, and I crept back rather foolishly. What would be the point of blowing up a lone stranger in an empty park? I unbuckled the bag, and gasped.

It was full of banknotes. Banknotes the foreigners had evidently intended me to have, been afraid I might not accept. What was I to do, except take the spoils home?

My wife was drying her hands on a towel in the kitchen. "Been out to collect the dole?" she asked scathingly.

I slid the bag across the table towards her. "Open it," I said.

Her eyes and mouth became three round O's in a startled, incredulous face.

"Fairy godmother gave it to me," I quipped. She wasn't impressed. "Spoke no English. Man, actually. He and his

daughter, or carer, insisted I keep it, and ran off. We're rich—
I think."

"You'll have to take it to the police," she whispered. "It can't
be ours. It's lost, or laundered, or whatever they call it when
keeping it's criminal."

"And say what? 'A stranger gave me all this money. I don't
want it'? They'll arrest me for theft, or a bad conscience, or
something."

"*You'd* never be brave enough to pull off a heist," she
scoffed, with some asperity.

I ignored this. "He's probably an eccentric millionaire, who
just took a fancy to me. Mind you, it could be ransom money:
they may be foreign dignitaries whose relative's been
kidnapped, and they've made the drop in the wrong park to
the wrong person! That would be a hoot, wouldn't it?"

"Yes," she cried, "when the kidnappers come after you!"

"How would they find out that we've got it?"

"Even if they don't, the police will. They'll trace those notes
as soon as we try to spend any of them and be on to us like a
ton of bricks."

"All the more reason we daren't go to the police. Besides, a
windfall is a windfall. We'll lie low till we're contacted, and if
not, it's 'Open sesame!' to Aladdin's cave!"

"To a prison cell, more likely," she said darkly.

I hid the bag in a bedroom cupboard and every day we
waited anxiously for a thunderous knock on the door, and
looked in the newspapers for news of a robbery or a
kidnapped foreign diplomat. But all that happened was that
we grew more and more troubled and dispirited. The thought
of all that money we couldn't spend lying there, and every car
or stranger in the street outside making us jump out of our
skins unnerved us, and we got crotchety and cross with each
other.

"We haven't had a decent outing in months," my wife complained. "I need new shoes and a new dress and it's high time we replaced the curtains in the living room. You've no job, no credit, just a bag of someone else's purloined cash you daren't spend. *You're* the hoot, you are!"

I was explaining we couldn't yet risk advertising our good fortune, when we heard the dreaded thunderous knock, and on the doorstep stood the expected policeman with all the weight of the law behind him.

"All right, officer," I said wearily, "we've got the money."

"Oh, good, because otherwise I must cut off your electricity. Overdue bill, sir."

"It's the electricity man," I said, staggering back indoors, weak at the knees.

"I can't stand this," my wife exclaimed. "Do something, or I'll not be here when you return!"

The river beyond the park was flowing swiftly after recent rains. Surreptitiously I launched the bag into midstream, and watched the burden of our wealth swept away, to make someone else happy, or sink and leave everyone no worse off than they had been.

Being rich certainly had made a difference. When I got home, I found my wife had absconded for an extended and possibly permanent outing with her mother.

5

The Siege of Rochester Castle

There are three square towers and one round one at the corners of Rochester Castle. Originally all four were square, until besieging soldiers conceived the idea of undermining one of them.

His protective leather jerkin was too cumbersome to wear in the narrow tunnel where Alfred was digging. Dank earth, roots, boulders, and airless darkness impeded his efforts as, crouching on his knees, he hammered away at the foundation stone he was prising loose. As he levered it out other workmen were waiting with ropes to haul it up from the hole where the tunnel began and roll in the heavy barrel which

Alfred, grunting and sweating, had somehow to prop in its place.

There were several such tunnels, with miners scrabbling like moles inside them, caked with dirt and mud. The entrance to each was protected by soldiers with shields over their heads to defend themselves against missiles shot or dropped upon them from the battlements above.

"What are they trying to do, up against the wall below us?" the rebellious Baron asked his son.

"I think they're trying to raise a ladder, but our defenders will easily stop them climbing the tower," the young man replied.

"The greedy King will have to do better than that," scoffed the Baron. "I will never pay the taxes he demands. If only it were Prince Arthur's army (but he's disappeared and nobody seems to know what's become of him) instead of the King's foreign mercenaries who've sailed over from France we'd soon see to it he didn't keep breaking the Great Charter he signed in our favour a few months ago!"

Surveying the siege from a safe distance, the King, conscious that he still had lots more barons' lands to devastate, reminded his philosopher, who was engineering the attack, "You have one week in which to force the Baron's surrender, or all your joints will be dislocated."

"It is well known," replied the philosopher placidly, "that all objects desire to reach their natural resting place, which, in the case of tower walls, is upon the element of earth below. Unsupported, they will seek the journey downwards, and the Baron will capitulate."

"Will the tower not fall on our miners while they are busy, or have we numbers enough to spare?"

"That is a hazard," the philosopher admitted, "but we have requisitioned all the pigs we could find on the surrounding farms, and they are being slaughtered in the camp."

"You will save the miners by sacrificing pigs? To what—to demons?" asked the King in alarm. "We daren't! Wrath will befall us! I forbid such wicked rites."

"Not to demons," the philosopher assured him soothingly, "but to the element of fire, which naturally rises, and will lift the tower till the miners have crawled out from under it."

"If that is so, you are a great magician," said the King.

Richard, the Baron's son, inspecting the lowest storey of the threatened tower, heard muffled voices and the sounds of hammering beneath his feet. Hastily he ordered his men to take up a section of the wooden floor, exposing the stones set in the earth below, to forestall what he concluded was an attempt to enter the tower from underground. A flagstone below the dismantled planks rocked when Richard stood on it, and the next moment he found himself hanging danger-ously on to the broken edge of the floor as the stone sank suddenly beneath him into the excavated hollow beneath. There was a scream as Alfred, unable to wriggle backwards quickly enough, was pinned under it. At the same time the lines of larded tow attached to the barrels of pig fat were ignited by the engineer at the tunnel entrances, and the miners, all but Alfred, crawled hastily out. Smoke and an acrid stench began to rise through the hole in the floor.

"Back to the top, men!" Richard shouted. "They're trying to burn us!"

Soon there was a raging conflagration beneath the tower, but the defenders had reached the battlements before the barrels of fat supporting the undermined walls had burnt sufficiently to bring the whole massive pile tumbling down in a jumbled ruin of dust and masonry. The screams of falling men were lost in the roar of the implosion. Richard's own despairing cry mingled with theirs, signalling only a moment's panic as he plunged incredulously earthwards in the midst of the disintegrating building.

The Baron in the castle keep heard the rumble and came out on to the wall to see the damage. "Impossible!" he exclaimed in amazement. "Doubtless some scion of Merlin's, who is known to have been engendered by a demon, is helping the King, in which case resistance is vain. Richard—where is Richard to carry out the flag of surrender?"

"Gone with the tower, sir," said a man-at-arms apologetically, before pitching over the battlements with an arrow through his throat.

The Baron grimaced, and gave the dismal order to raise the portcullis. "Richard's was a noble death," he said, "and we will rebuild the tower as a monument to him, when this accursed King John has decamped, with his purses bulging with as little tax as we can persuade him to accept."

"All the defenders of the castle, Baron, knights, bowmen, varlets, the lot, must be put to death," the King insisted.

"Sire, bethink yourself," counselled the philosopher. "Be content with the slaughter only of the cooks and scullery boys, or the people of England will be so incensed that they will destroy our whole foreign army. Then how shall we reduce the rest of the barons?"

"The new tower," the Baron meanwhile was deciding thoughtfully, "must be round, like the course of the sun across the heavens. Demons have no power over the circular spheres above the changeable moon. And even on earth a curved wall sends arrows and spears glancing aside as square walls do not."

6

Pepys' Ghost

When we were children my brother and I were afraid of ghosts. The mysterious creaks and groans one heard if one was unlucky enough to wake up in the middle of the night could only be made by ghosts, and the only recourse was to bury one's trembling self under the blankets and fervently hope one would go back to sleep as quickly as possible.

"You could imagine the ghost of a person—" my father explained,

"Don't tell them that!" Mother interjected.

"No, wait," Father continued, "but you couldn't imagine ghosts of clothes, could you? Therefore every ghost ought to be stark naked!"

He was wrong, but he made us laugh, and the ridicule relieved our tension, for a while.

One night I looked out of the window and saw a white shirt Mother had left on the washing line flapping about in the wind. "Look," I said to my nervous younger brother, "there's a white ghost dancing around outside."

He was too young to disbelieve anything he was told, and set up a frightened wailing, which brought a solicitous parent into the room to console him and rebuke me for being mischievous.

Some time later we went on holiday somewhere, and in the course of the journey spent a night at an old inn called the Pepys' Arms. Why that portion of his anatomy should have been so singled out I couldn't understand, but I was interested because I'd recently heard about him, the Saviour of the Navy who'd written a diary in code, in a history lesson at school.

The inn had managed to avoid demolition for hundreds of years. It had low ceilings, great black beams, and narrow, twisting stairs that creaked as we went up to bed, my brother and I in a tiny attic that fortunately opened out of the larger room where our parents slept, in a huge four-poster with curtains they could actually draw if they'd wanted to. When we'd investigated this phenomenon thoroughly enough to be irritating, we were packed off to the less interesting but delightfully snug twin beds next door, where my brother gave last-minute instructions that the light was by no means to be turned out, in case he needed to call anyone in the night. I had assured him that the inn must be simply full of ghosts, which would all come crowding into the room as soon as we tried to go to sleep.

I woke up, unsure where I was, fascinated by the fitful moonlight seeping through the little leaded panes in the window. There was no other light, but I could see the open doorway into our parents' room, and through it, quite plainly, came a man in seventeenth-century costume, with a thick brown wig over his head, hanging in rich curls down to his shoulders. I knew him at once, for we had been shown a picture of him in the history lesson at school.

"Good evening, Mr Pepys," I said politely, not at all surprised that he should be there.

He bowed, but said nothing, and went on walking slowly between our two beds.

"Please don't wake my little brother," I said. "He's terribly afraid of ghosts."

Mr Pepys only smiled, and moved sedately on, to disappear, somewhere or somehow, through a wall, perhaps. I congratulated myself that now that I was bigger and braver, Mr Pepys had proved that ghosts were not frightening after all, even if they did walk through one's bedroom at night.

My father came into the room. "I heard you talking," he said. "Are you all right?"

"I saw Mr Pepys," I explained.

"Did you? Well, he's gone now. Lie down and go back to sleep, and it will soon be morning. He won't come back."

But he did, and spent all night sitting on my bed telling me how he'd left a whole library of valuable books to be looked after in Cambridge, and in spite of all the years that had passed his instructions were still being followed to the letter. I think that's what he talked about: I can't be sure exactly.

As the cheery proprietress was serving breakfast next morning, I told her solemnly that I had seen Mr Pepys walk through our attic bedroom. "He talked to me for a long time, though I can't quite remember what he said. But he was careful not to waken my brother."

25

"That was thoughtful of him, dear. But I'm sure he was a kind man."

"I did see him," I insisted, for no one seemed to believe me.

"Very likely," she answered, smiling. "Oh, Mr Pepys, and no doubt his wife too, often slept here. That's why the inn is called the Pepys' Arms. In fact, there's a picture of him on the wall there."

I looked where she pointed; I hadn't noticed the picture before.

"Yes," I said, "he looked exactly like that."

"Don't talk nonsense," my father said tersely. "There's no such thing as ghosts!"

As I looked away from the picture Mr Pepys winked at me. Clear as anything. I smiled as I returned to my corn flakes. No such thing as ghosts? He and I knew better!

Years later, I returned to the inn, just to make sure, perhaps, that it was still there. It was a fascinating old place, but by no means so eerie as I remembered it. The picture of Mr Pepys still hung on the wall, rather dismal and dusty now, and from whatever angle I looked at it, I could not persuade myself that Mr Pepys winked.

7

Not to be Exported

During the war many countries not actively involved in hostilities sent young volunteers to the front lines or on to ships patrolling ocean routes threatened by submarines. At ten years old Alan did not understand why notices at all the railway stations sternly enjoined, "Don't talk about ships or shipping," but concluded that he must at all costs keep secret the fact that the Lower Road Primary School he attended had adopted a ship, the *Jason,* and regularly sent food parcels to the sailors on board.

On month-end Monday the teacher instructed her pupils to help their parents aid the war effort by bringing a tin of food

or a grocery packet to school. These the keenest girls would assiduously pack into the parcel that was to be sent to the *Jason*, while the boys got in the way or played the fool behind the teacher's back.

Joan, the girl Alan dared not admit that he liked best, because the boys would tease him, suddenly held up a tin evidently intended for local consumption, and read the label in an excited treble: "It says 'Not to be Exported'!"

"Oh, that doesn't mean we can't send it to the ship," the teacher dismissively replied. But surely it did? Joan knew what the word meant, increasing Alan's admiration for her, and so did he, because his uncle had a shop that in some mysterious way was badly affected by imports and exports. War for Alan meant keeping secrets and, now, changing the meaning of words if it suited the war effort.

Joan, sadly, soon left Lower Road and was lost sight of in an all-girls' school, so that it was many years before Alan saw her again. The war was over, but imports and exports were still a major cause of concern to the country and particularly to his uncle's state of mind. Quite by accident Alan got a job in the same draper's business where Joan worked, he in gents' ties and socks, she in ladies' hats. He wasn't sure he recognized her; she was too anxious to please her employers to acknowledge his tentative greeting with an open show of recognition.

All the more so because at tea-break when his feet involuntarily took him to inspect the ladies' hats he found her in conversation with a young fellow she reluctantly introduced as Keith. Keith, it seemed, had actually lunched with her at her parents' home, was a Johnny-come-lately who was already a half-accepted suitor, and now proved anxious to describe to this former school-fellow of hers, Alan, something of the inevitable course of their relationship.

At the end of the working day Joan smiled somewhat wistfully (did she?) at Alan, and then tossed her head as Keith led her by the hand down the stairs and out of the building.

Ex porta—out of the door. Alan shrugged, and in future harboured among the ties and socks.

Some years later, in a new job issuing motor licences, Alan found himself dealing with an application from Joan's father, containing not only the family's present address, but the information that he was planning shortly to emigrate. Was his daughter still with that Keith—they were surely too young to have married! but one never knew, these days—or might it be possible to see her again before she followed her father irretrievably into the unknown?

Amazed at his own temerity, Alan knocked at her father's door.

"I—er—had to pass this way, and thought I'd deliver your motor-licence personally—sir," he stammered, when the man himself half-opened the door and frowned enquiringly at him.

"Thank you. They usually post it."

"I—I understand you're emigrating, sir."

"Considering it."

"I think—I mean, I *was*, at school with your daughter. Joan."

"Indeed? You are—?"

Alan gave his name. The alarming face relaxed in a brief smile. "Come in," he said.

Her mother was sitting in the living room. She glanced at him a trifle bleakly, Alan thought.

"I knew Joan," Alan explained awkwardly. "I thought I'd call, to—to say goodbye."

"Goodbye, yes. That's kind of you." She sighed.

"You'll be taking her with you, I suppose?"

"Oh no, no chance of that." Her mother gave a wry smile.

No chance! Joan was not to be exported! Then he remembered Keith, and Alan's leaping heart sank.

"I met a young man with her. Keith," he said nervously.

"Keith was killed in the accident," she replied. "You heard about the accident? Of course: that's why you're here. She won't know you, I'm afraid. The doctors have given her only a few days. The hospital needed the bed, so we're looking after her in her own home, with a nurse at night."

Alan could not speak. His mouth opened and shut. He felt cold all over. He had to get out, before he screamed, or collapsed. He turned and rushed from the room, and the house.

Joan, *his* Joan, not Keith's, not theirs. He had known her nearly all her life. A *few days*, and then to be exported for ever! Just when he had found her, she would not know him!

A week, ten days, passed. He was back at work, miserably, mechanically. Life must go on, after all, for those that remain. But an *accident*, that a split second might have avoided!

And then a message came, the envelope marked from her father. Tremblingly he opened it. Would it contain news of the funeral? The first line blinded his eyes with tears.

"Joan seems to be making a remarkable recovery. The doctors are amazed at her powers of resilience. Restoration will take a long time, of course, but she is grateful you came to see her, *and would like to thank you personally whenever* ..."

Alan leapt from his chair and punched the air with a yell of triumph.

8

A Stitch in Time

Pitting his driving skills against the twists and switch-back dips of the track through the Central African bush, Max Benson drove as fast as the bucking wheels of his car would permit, hoping to reach town before nightfall. The road, he reckoned, would have been better maintained in colonial times. Every few hundred yards among the crooked trees anthills bulged from the red clay, like carbuncles on a hirsute face, some huge enough to support a small grove of trees, others barely knee high, but all indicative of thousands, perhaps millions, of years of industrious activity far outstripping that of the human builders of more recent times.

A truck dimly visible through a cloud of dust slowed his progress as he rounded another bend. It was impossible to pass, and he had to hope that the driver would take pity on him and slew off the road when the track widened sufficiently. Fortunately, at last, the truck pulled into a cleared space in front of a village shop. Benson saw men leaping from the open back; they seemed to be armed. He drove on hastily, for the troubles had not ceased with the attainment of independence: clashes between supporters of rival politicians were frequent.

A village meant there must be a river nearby, and almost immediately he found himself at the top of a steep bank down which the road cheerfully plunged. Larger gullies were usually bridged, though sometimes the planks had been stripped or destroyed during the worst of the troubles. The stream at the bottom of this bank, however, seemed to be shallow enough, in the dry season at least, for most vehicles to negotiate, for the road continued up the opposite bank, but there were naked boys swimming in the water. They scuttled out of the way and waved him through, but Benson dared not risk being stuck in the middle. So he alighted, took off his shoes and, reluctantly, since sluggish pools where village children played were a typical breeding ground for the snails that carried bilharzia, waded back and forth to test the depth of the ford. Satisfied, he drove at a rush down the slope, sending up twin curtains of spray as his tyres squelched through the mud at the bottom, and then revved fiercely up the steep side opposite. There his engine spluttered and died.

He climbed ruefully out, and soon there was a concourse of villagers round the stationary car, peering as uncomprehendingly into the engine as Benson was doing himself.

"You are anxious to spend the night in the car?" someone asked helpfully, offering Benson the ragged blanket he was too evidently in the habit of sleeping in himself.

"We cook this for you," suggested the shopkeeper, precariously balancing a tin of bully-beef on a chipped saucer.

"No thank you, but I would like a cup of tea," Benson smiled, relieved to find them friendly.

The request seemed to cause consternation, from one end of the village to the other, until the shopkeeper produced a pound of best blend, which he gave to his uncomprehending wife to deal with. She tore it open and advanced meaningfully towards a boiling cauldron on an outside stove. Benson hastily took over, before she tipped the whole packetful into a pot large enough to fill a small bath.

At the other end of the village there was a sudden commotion, as an altercation developed between the truckload of recent arrivals and political opponents in the huts round about. Soon the reloaded truck splashed through the stream, shrilly abused by the children floundering about nearby, roared past his stranded car, and swept noisily away into the distance. But the yelling continued, and soon a matronly woman, screaming in a language Benson did not understand, came rushing up waving her arms.

Benson found himself summoned by the men around him, and excitedly urged to follow the woman. "You come, man stabbed!" the shopkeeper explained.

"I'm not a doctor!" he cried, but no one believed he had not magic enough to assist the wounded person, who was writhing on the ground, bleeding from a deep gash in his arm.

"Tourniquet," Benson muttered, falling on his knees beside the patient. He knotted his handkerchief as tightly as he could above the wound, but it obviously needed stitches and bandaging. Squeezing the flesh together he signalled urgently for bandaging and—well, why not? he thought—a needle and thread, if the anguished man would allow him to use it.

"He die, we kill," someone warningly said.

"Hold him down," Benson said grimly, as, gritting his teeth, he passed the needle through the gaping skin. Loss of blood had reduced the victim to a gibbering wreck, and Benson was able to complete the job, and then bandage the lacerated bicep till his unsightly handiwork was no longer visible.

Unsteadily but proudly he fetched a tin of water from the cauldron to wash the blood from his hands. There was more of it than he had realized. It seemed to cake his arms half way up to the elbows. But he had, surely, saved the man's life. The engine, he found, had dried sufficiently to be re-started, but he was not permitted to drive away alone. The patient was lifted into the back, his wife, the woman who had screamed, wedged herself in beside him, and the shopkeeper piled into the passenger seat in front.

"You drive hospital," he said.

"Man not recover, you die," the Banshee voice of one of the onlookers repeated.

Reaching the town, Benson delivered his passengers to the hospital, and, well pleased with the conclusion of his adventure, drove happily on his way.

It was a couple of weeks later that he became ill.

"Bilharzia?" he asked anxiously.

"No," the doctor grimly answered. "It's ebola."

9

The Housemaster

Being a housemaster at a rowdy boys' school was not the kindest initiation into his chosen profession for a young teacher like Reginald. Anxious to impress his colleagues and imagining that his self-respect demanded that he keep tight control over the boys in his charge, he found himself the natural butt of youngsters only a little younger than himself, who treated him at best with tolerance and at worst with contempt.

A climax came when three masters from a school up country brought their entire complement of football teams to spend Friday night in one of the dormitories at Reginald's

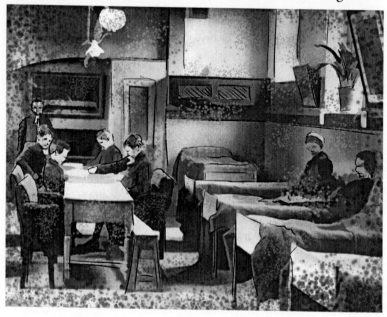

hostel before they played their scheduled matches against the local school on Saturday. The masters went off to enjoy half the night at various places of entertainment in the town, and left Reginald in *de facto* charge.

Knitting his brows when the noise became unbearable, he ventured into the long bedroom full of excited holiday-makers, and tried to suppress the turbulence. He might have been King Canute proving he had no power to stem an incoming tide.

"Tell him," someone said, and a deputation advanced upon him out of the hullabaloo. He cringed inwardly: what did they expect him to do? He had just failed to arrest a skater who was cannoning from wall to wall down the corridor. "One of our chaps has been beaten up!"

Was the whole dormitory, then, seething at this provocation to war? How was Reginald, of all people, to prevent a mass charge of alien footballers to battle with local innocents in the other dormitories? A way of escape presented itself, in the bruised face of the lad who had been beaten. He had a black eye, a swollen cheekbone, and a cut lip. As a drowning man clutches at a straw, Reginald marched him outside to his car, and drove him away to the hospital.

In a distressingly short time a doctor pronounced the injuries superficial, and a nurse patched the lad up with ointments and soothing words. Reginald was forced to bring him straight back to the hostel. It was alarmingly quiet, but neither on fire nor sporting broken windows, nor were the corridors littered with boys with broken heads. Could he be court-marshalled, or whatever the equivalent was for housemasters who deserted their post?

Mr Jameson, the hostel superintendent, had come from his quarters to preside over the abandoned boys, who, chastened and subdued, were preparing for bed.

"It sounded like a riot," he told Reginald. "You weren't here!"

Reginald swallowed. Jameson turned his attention to the beaten boy. "What happened to you?"

Contritely, the boy explained. "Some of us went down town. I know we weren't supposed to, but we thought ourselves more adult than we were. We met a fellow with his girlfriend, who told us to *stick around*. I said something I shouldn't have, trying to be clever, and he started punching me, to show off in front of his girlfriend. Apparently he was a boxer, which didn't help me."

"What did you say?" the superintendent wanted to know.

"I'd rather not tell you," the embarrassed boy replied.

But, to Reginald's surprise, Jameson insisted.

"I said," the boy awkwardly admitted, "Stick her somewhere else!"

Jameson nodded. "I'm not surprised he punched you. He was my best boxer in the hostel when he was at school a few years ago. Reckon you've learnt your lesson?"

"Yes, sir."

"Right lads, five minutes to lights out!"

The prefect who had apparently helped the superintendent quell the riot spoke up. "Seeing we're on holiday, sir, we normally have an extra half-hour, sir."

Jameson fixed him with a steely glare, and said, "I think they've forfeited it, don't you? Three minutes now!"

Reginald's heart sank. How would they deal with the chorus of objections that surely must follow? But the prefect subsided abashed, and there was no sound but the hasty donning of pyjamas and the creak of beds under rustling blankets.

"An extra half-hour, to let them start up again?" the superintendent snorted, as he and Reginald went downstairs. "You did right to take the boy to out-patients. Silly young ass!"

"I thought he came out of it rather well," Reginald ventured.

"Oh, yes, good material there! This could be just the wake-up call he needed."

"How did you manage to quieten them, Mr Jameson?" Reginald was emboldened to ask.

"Oh, I sent a boy to winkle out the prefect for me, and told him to go round telling the lads to settle down, which he hadn't thought it within his province to do earlier." Reginald's lips tightened. Affecting not to notice, Jameson went on, "Then I stood silently in the doorway looking as if I'd eat the next boy who stepped out of line. Actually, I think they were rather frightened by what had happened to the chap you took to hospital." He laughed. "For all they knew, that might have been my favourite form of punishment!"

Next morning at breakfast one of Reginald's younger colleagues asked curiously, "What was all that noise about last night?"

Reginald coloured, and murmured something. Was this to be the accusation of incompetence he dreaded?

"I wasn't going to show myself," the other asserted. "I don't know how you coped! Thank goodness you were on duty, I thought. I hope Jameson reads the riot act to those masters of theirs, leaving you to face their hooligans alone! In fact," he added, looking darkly at the skulking three, self-consciously downing bacon and eggs at a separate table, "if I were Jameson I'd write their headmaster a real snorter of a complaint!" He shook his head admiringly at Reginald. "How you managed I can't imagine! I'm sure I couldn't have."

"Oh," said Reginald airily. "Merely high spirits! They only needed to have a little authority shown them. Good fellows, most of them!"

10

The Hollow Ball

A titled aristocrat, impoverished by repeated death duties, brought a stone or metal sphere, about the size of a baby's fist, to show an antique dealer. Family records, he said, indicated that it had been dug up in 1796 by an ancestor planting potatoes in a corner of the ancient vegetable garden that had once belonged to a medieval monastery. It was greyish with indecipherable markings on its otherwise smooth surface, heavier than lead, and faintly warm when held in the hand.

"I cannot guess its value," admitted the dealer, after examining it through his strongest magnifying glass and

finding it too hard to scratch even with a diamond cutter, "but leave it with me, and I'll make enquiries."

This its owner was obliged to do, and the dealer took it to a friend, who happened to be a professor of cosmological physics. Even after thorough examination in the University laboratories, the Professor was unable to determine its composition.

"I think it must be part of a meteorite," he told his technician. "If only we could examine the site where it landed! But who knows where the old monks who lost it in their garden got it from? Any records they may have left were long since destroyed by Thomas Cromwell's iconoclasm."

A team of investigators became more and more puzzled as their tests proceeded. Its temperature remained constant whether it was placed in super-heated fire or in dry ice, and an electron microscope revealed that its surface molecules were so tightly packed that they scarcely responded to the most extreme of outside influences. Maps were made of its markings, which were projected on a screen and presented to academic audiences world wide, but no one could say either how they had been made or what, if anything, they meant.

Romantics talked as if scientists now had proof that advanced alien civilizations existed and were sending messages round the cosmos, and crank alarmists speculated that a spy satellite from outer space had been planted among the inhabitants of earth.

"Except that it can only have been manufactured in the glowing heart of some exploding supernova, we cannot guess how it was made," suggested the cosmologist poetically. It was a young student who came up with a theory, ridiculed at first, which eventually caught the imagination of academe. "The markings," he said, studying the maps that had been made of them, "are continents! And," he added, when supporters for his idea began to crop up, "could we see below the surface, impossible at present, we should find other markings, other continents, and so on down to the core, like hieroglyphics on the skins of an onion or—"

"Or," opined a classical philosopher, "like the Ptolemaic model of the universe, which posited a terrestrial centre surrounded by seven planetary spheres."

"Ah!" said the cosmologist, in wonder. "Can Ptolemy supersede Copernicus?"

"What's going on?" the owner of the ball demanded. "Is it valuable or not?"

"Sit down," said the cosmologist, "and listen quietly while I explain what we have determined this ball to be, incredible though it will sound." He gasped and seemed to have difficulty finding his next words. "It is a solar system from some far galaxy, compressed by its own imploding weight into what is known as a black hole, which, having absorbed all the matter it could contain, is now so solid that it has become inactive, and in some past age was swept on quantum tides of dark matter until it fell to earth. For all we know, it may, when it did so, have caused the moon to break away from this world, or brought about the extinction of the dinosaurs."

The owner shrugged. "What can I sell it for?" he asked.

"Oh, you can't. It belongs to all mankind. It will sit in the British Museum, requisitioned by the Nation for a nominal sum, unless the Americans outbid us and snaffle it for the Smithsonian."

Suddenly his cellphone chimed, and his mouth fell open as he listened to the excited chatter of his technician. "Spots the size of a pinhead have been detected that are hotter, by millionths of a degree, than the surrounding areas. And warming, even as I speak. Volcanoes!"

"Nothing can escape a black hole! Eruptions are impossible!" the cosmologist cried.

"This one is becoming active again, but backwards. Can you imagine what the energy in the core of that thing must be like, if any of it should get out?"

"No!" the Professor exclaimed. "I must phone the Prime Minister. We must jet-plane it to the most powerful rocket launcher the Americans or North Koreans, or anybody, may have ready for blastoff! But it will take years, perhaps centuries, to travel far enough away to save us from Total Annihilating Compression and Smithereens if—no, when—it goes off!"

"Don't be daft!" said the owner. "Just pay up and shut up!"

"It's a fake," scoffed M.I.T. scientists. "An imploded solar system would be so heavy it would fall straight through the centre of the earth!"

Then news came that it had burst. The outer skin was less than a nanometre thick. Inside was nothing: it was not only empty, but its depths looked immeasurable.

"*Creatio ex nihilo!*" proclaimed a Latinist. "Matter from nothing. Not from empty space, but from nowhere, where not even emptiness existed."

"Stranger still," the technician reported, "anything inserted, a light, or a probe, simply and finally disappears. If we can discover why, we may find a solution to the disposal of nuclear waste!"

Then over his cellphone he shrieked, "Anything near it vanishes too! It's emptying the laboratory! It's—Ahh!"

The cosmologist went white as a ghost. "It's reversing itself! Our experiments have unleashed not the Big Bang, or the Big Whimper, but the Grand Syphon! It will absorb all matter back into nothing! How long before we disappear, returned to pre-creatorial non-existence? How long will it take to nullify the universe? How l—"

11

Number Eleven

Eleven, fascinating number, one that had caught Sebastian's fancy! 11, like stilts, or legs just beginning to step out towards adulthood and independence, the age Gillian, that daughter of a neighbour's of his, had been when she disappeared all those years ago, and the number of the mysterious house just down the road from where Sebastian lived.

He had often wondered who lived there, and what went on behind the tall railings and the trees that masked its gloomy walls, especially in summer when the leaves were thickest. He took to pacing up and down the street in front of it, for

morning or afternoon exercise, but it remained as silent and uncommunicative as ever. Very occasionally he saw the owner emerge, and carefully lock the iron gates behind him; a dowdy man in an old brown coat and cloth cap, whose forbidding frown was not neighbourly. He had tried to greet him, and received only a curt nod in reply, before the man hurried away with his shopping bag on his arm.

Once when he had gone Sebastian caught a glimpse, he thought, of a young woman flitting amongst the trees. She wore a long grey dress and bonnet, glanced briefly towards the gate, but her face was too much in shadow to be seen clearly, and quickly disappeared through the dark portal of the house.

"Morning, Mr Tansly!" Sebastian greeted the man as he was unlocking his gate. "Much sunnier out in the open than under all those trees you've got in front of your house!"

"Why are you always loitering about here?" Tansly growled. "I don't like it!"

"I live just down the road," Sebastian answered, aggrieved. "I'm almost sure I saw a young lady on your property recently, but I've never seen her walking in the street."

"Almost sure!" Tansly snorted. "There's no young lady. I live alone." He relocked the gate, and strode indignantly indoors.

"I wouldn't be surprised if he's got that missing child Gillian locked up in there," Sebastian told his aunt, who lived with him.

"Then you should go to the police, dear," his aunt said. "But she's dead long since, I've no doubt."

"It's a serious allegation, sir," the policeman in the charge office told Sebastian.

"A hunch, not an allegation," Sebastian protested, "but one you should investigate, in the case of a surly character like Tansly."

The police did call, and were angrily dismissed. "If you keep pestering me," Tansly fumed, meeting Sebastian next day, "I'll bring an action against you for harassment!"

Was that a frightened face at a window, or did Sebastian imagine it, as he looked over Tansly's shoulder?

"You'll have to get a warrant, and make a thorough search," he insisted at the charge office. "He says he lives alone, but I saw someone in the house!"

How Tansly raged when he was forced to permit the search Sebastian did not hear, but was informed in due course that his suspicions were without foundation. The face he had seen belonged to Tansly's sister, who was a reclusive invalid in a wheelchair, and therefore unknown in the neighbourhood. There was quite certainly no one else in the house.

"If she's in a wheelchair, she couldn't have been flitting among the trees like the girl I glimpsed," Sebastian told his aunt. "Perhaps they keep her locked up most of the time in a cellar or attic behind a secret door somewhere!"

"If the police say there's no one there, we should believe them. You're too inquisitive: it's none of our business who may be living in that house," his aunt said.

"We'll have to be more careful about letting her out," Tansly told his sister, "with that fellow nosing around all the time!"

"They won't find her," his sister said. "They missed the trapdoor under the bookcase. She's much too frightened of the outside world to go near the railings, and far too dependant upon us to be anything but useful to me. 'Gillian,' I'll tell her, 'if you see a man peering into our garden, stay out of sight. He would want to take you away from us, and you know what happens to young women when men like that take them away!' Oh, that will make her shudder all right!"

Sebastian wasn't satisfied, and climbing cautiously over the railing one night went all round the house attempting to see through the darkened windows. He even tried the back door, but not surprisingly, it was locked.

Next day, however, the police were summoned, and Tansly's body was found in the garden, stabbed repeatedly with a kitchen knife that was still embedded in one of the wounds.

"Oh, aunt, aunt!" Gillian cried, throwing herself on the floor in front of the sister's chair and clasping her about the knees. "He jumped at me under the trees, and tried to—to—I only wanted to push him off. I've no idea how I came to be holding the knife!"

"You imagined it, dear," said the woman, her eyes glittering dangerously. "You couldn't have stabbed him: he'd have stopped you at the first thrust. Some dreadful intruder got in, and my poor brother went outside to confront him. Don't worry! You won't need to live in the cellar any more, unless you want to. You can sleep in the little room next to mine, and look after me as you always do so well. I'll send for my niece Tilly to do the shopping for us. We'll tell her, and the detective if he calls again, that you're a new companion who can't leave me."

"Oh, I'm much too frightened to ever dare leave you!"

"I know, dear. And you won't have to."

The detective, in due course, called on Sebastian also. "There was an intruder on the property that night," he said. "We found plenty of footprints, and they weren't Mr Tansly's. What size are your boots, sir? Size eleven? I thought so!"

12

The Biscuit Factory

"In my grandfather's time," said the derelict, lying on plastic bags against the graffiti-defaced wall of the empty factory building, "this place was teeming like an ants' nest. Lemon creams were his speciality, and he churned them out at a rate you wouldn't believe. You couldn't name an interstate that didn't have one or more of his lorries loaded to the roof with the nation's favourite cookie, trundling them along to every outlet from here to California!"

"Lemon creams, eh?" said the social worker, looking up at the blackened and broken walls of the half-demolished building. "What are they?"

"What indeed? Can't be had here or anywhere the way he made them. And why? Because of the education he gave his son, my father. It all came of hankering after royalty, and trying to make up for what happened at Concord Bridge."

"What do you mean?" asked the social worker, squatting down in front of the tramp.

"He sent him across the Atlantic, to gain *his* independence, he said. An independent school in England would be the making of him, he thought, without thinking of what it would make him, and they stuck him in one of their ancient public schools instead, assuring him that's what they call independent schools over there. And what did he learn? That cookies are called biscuits. He came back determined to turn this flourishing factory into a biscuit factory, and ruined my prospects by doing it!"

"I don't see what the difference was," the social worker said mildly.

"The difference was that between success and disaster. They taught him, in the land of kings and chefs, that biscuit means twice cooked. I ask you! Bis, he would say, is twice, well, that's fair enough, I guess, or I suppose, as they'd say over there, and the rest of it comes from an ancient language (they insist on anything ancient over there, to make up for losing the New world) according to which it means cooked. Like their brains, I guess."

"Yes, but how did that affect your inheritance?"

"Well, he said Queen Victoria liked them twice cooked, and he was going to have Queen Victoria's taste spread all over the States! Anything royal, you see, would sell like—like biscuits, to atone for what the Minute Men did at Concord. So he took grandfather's much desired cookies, and—cooked them again!"

"And that did it, did it?"

"Changed the flavour, colour, and consistency. Made them hard, black and charcoaly. Orders fell off. Customers wanted cookies, not Queen Victoria. He had to start laying off workers. When part of the factory fell into disrepair, he couldn't afford to repair it. Never mind how he advertised, never mind that he'd re-introduced the real royal biscuit to suit the discerning palate, fewer and fewer people wanted to discern it. Eventually we went out of business."

"We?"

"Well, there was nothing left for me, was there, after my father's pig-headedness? Thousands of dollars worth, I should have been. But," the tramp added, smiling, "I'm thinking of righting the ancient wrong, of restoring the factory, my grandfather's legacy, and America's favourite tea-time snack!"

"And how," asked the social worker, seeing here signs of a willingness to be uplifted that gave him hope the tramp might be reclaimed, "do you plan to do that?"

"By attracting investment. Advertising, machine hire, employing a workforce, acquiring ingredients, restoring this factory building, which needs a little smartening up, you'll agree, will all take time, and, unfortunately, dollars. So I'm looking for investment. Now if you would care to invest, say, five thousand dollars, I could assure you of substantial returns once we get the business going. No? A thousand would help me to start. Five hundred?"

The social worker shook his head. "My job hasn't allowed me to accumulate capital," he said. "But here, I can let you have five dollars! But tomorrow I will want to know that you've laid them out responsibly."

"Oh, I'll do that all right," said the tramp, struggling to his feet. "A budding capitalist, on the threshold of a great enterprise, can't be expected to get going on an empty stomach. He needs his wits about him, and they require nourishment."

The philanthropist watched him lurch away, his newly acquired wealth concealed somewhere in the baggy breeches that hung from his emaciated waist, towards what the philanthropist hoped would not be a mainly sharp and liquid lunch.

13

The Lady, Not the Tiger

Frank Stockton's *The Lady, or the Tiger?* was one of the stories that unsettled my childhood, by its infuriating inconclusiveness. When the low-born lover opened the door in the amphitheatre indicated by his semi-barbaric princess, the bloodthirsty majority of the class, and our English master, and, I suspect, Frank Stockton too, were sure that out would spring the starving tiger, while the compassionate minority, of whom I was one, opted for the lady. Outvoted, I could only cringe in silence. Now, after all these years, it is my duty to prove that I was right.

I grant that the jealous hatred of a semi-barbaric princess for her rival could not have borne the sight of her fickle lover celebrating a joyous marriage right there in the amphitheatre before her furious eyes; that she had found out correctly which door concealed the lady and which the tiger, that she had conveyed the intelligence accurately to her lover, and that he had punctiliously followed her directions, and gone to the door on the right as she had indicated. Indeed, I do not doubt that she intended him to encounter the tiger. Yet I still maintain that, to her horror and indignation, out stepped the lady, and an answering cry of delight ascended from the tiers of excited onlookers as he clasped her rapturously in his arms.

Perhaps you think I shall try to argue that he was no fool (oh but he was, for he was in love!) and understood her semi-barbaric frame of mind, so that he deliberately chose the door she did not indicate. That of course is what you or I would have done, not being in love with the princess. But a true lover will obey his mistress's whims however fatal they may be: remember *The Glove and the Lions*? If not, read how a besotted lover spontaneously leapt into a lions' den to retrieve the glove his beloved had dropped, to test his gallantry.* The princess indicated the door on the right, and he went to the right accordingly.

Here then, *pace* Frank Stockton, who leaves the issue undecided, is what followed. Down from her semi-barbaric throne leapt the irate princess, when her hated rival emerged, and bounded with the athleticism of a tennis champion celebrating victory at Wimbledon into the arena. "This," she screamed, running to the unopened door and flinging it wide, "*this* was the door you were meant to open!"

There was a roar, a blur of muscular limb and tawny hide, a crunch and the voracious champ of greedy jaws, as the tiger devoured its victim, till only the skull, a few bones of the feet,

---

* See Leigh Hunt's poem, and how Robert Browning excuses the lady in his rejoinder "The Glove".

and what could not be licked out from inside the stained and shredded clothes were left.

Shocked out of her senses, the fainting lady still clung to her lover's arm as he solicitously supported her drooping body, while guards with pitchforks persuaded the now satisfied tiger to return to its cage, where, purring contentedly, it curled up and went to sleep.

"How," the lady gasped, upon recovering, "did you know which door I was waiting behind? Did you not follow her—its (with a shudder of distaste at the yet unswept remains)—directions?"

"I did. I certainly meant to," answered the bemused man, scratching his puzzled head.

"Oh, you meant to, did you? Never mind, you didn't know me then. But what can have happened? Did she pity you until she saw you with me, and then change her mind and hurtle down into the arena to bring out the tiger she wished she had selected?"

"No. She signalled with her right hand and rushed to the door on her right hand. That was the one she meant me to open, the one with the tiger behind it." He gave a sentimental sniff. "She loved me too much to want you to have me. You will have me, won't you?"

"Then why didn't you do as she wished?" the lady went on, ignoring his question as the answer was too obvious to need stating. "Will you pretend you saw through her dastardly scheme and deliberately disobeyed her?"

"Oh, no. She signalled with her right, but I was facing her, and imagined she meant the door on my right hand, and there I found you!" He smiled at the pretty face looking up at him, and kissed it.

"But," the lady objected, knitting her beautiful brows, "there's a flaw in this somewhere. You turned, didn't you?"

53

"Of course. I wasn't going to be staring like a nincompoop at the princess while I opened a door behind me! You'd have thought me a boorish idiot if you'd come out at my back and found I hadn't the courtesy to be facing you!"

"But then the tiger's door would have been on your right."

"Would it? I didn't think of that; I'd have been horribly confused if I had. But I didn't turn far enough. I thought she meant me to turn right, clockwise, and your door, the first I came to, was still on my right when I opened it."

"You mean, you didn't turn to the left, when the princess signalled to the right, as any sensible person would have done?"

"That wasn't my right."

"So you turned the wrong way round!"

"That's right."

"Right," said the lady with a sigh and a shake of the head, realizing it was stupidity, not cleverness or luck, that had saved her bridegroom. "I can see I'm going to have a right old time with this one!"

"Come on," she urged, seeing he was looking somewhat ruefully at what was left of the princess, "the wedding procession is about to begin. Keep clear of the King, in case he decides he'd rather have seen us devoured than his daughter!"

14

The Ring

What sort of story might a reader expect would follow a title such as this? Does it suggest a round ring, or a loud ring? Should it tell of a wedding ring, a boxing ring, or a bell ring? When an author cannot make up his mind, a reader is free to choose whichever best pleases him, or indeed, another kind of ring altogether, if he can think of one. Here, therefore, is an invitation to cooperate with an ambivalent author by perusing whichever of the following paragraphs seems most congenial.

First then, Helene waited eagerly with her trembling fourth finger extended for the best man fumbling in his fob pocket to

produce the ring that the groom was to thrust over her knuckle. Instead, there was a tinkle as the too hastily extracted ring bounced on to the floor of the church, and unerringly finding one of the many knot holes or cracks between the planks disappeared irretrievably into the darkness below. In vain did the diving bridesmaids and anxious groom fling themselves floorwards to grasp the glittering gold before it disappeared for ever; grimly and grimily they rose and dusted hands and knees; sadly wept the bride, fearing that without the giving of rings no marriage could be declared valid; contritely the abashed groomsman tried to excuse his clumsiness.

Upon the verandah of their house on a little hillock overlooking the churchyard Helene and her husband watched a group of children, their own three among them, playing around the gravestones. On a patch greener than the rest they clasped hands and singing "Ring a ring o' roses" danced in a circle until breathless and laughing they collapsed in a heap after the last line.

A rhyme thought to derive from the plague years, the roses being the pustules of the disease, the pocketful of posies an aromatic if ineffective prophylactic, the sneezes the body's last desperate attempt to rid itself of the murderous microbes, the collapse the sufferer's inevitable end.

"They're not getting up," cried Helene in consternation, leaping to her feet as the children remained motionless while time for her frozen brain seemed to stop.

The telephone rang. Not till the ringing ceased when her husband lifted the receiver did Helene breathe freely as she saw the first child sit up. Soon they were racing about as gaily as ever. But the man's face was serious when he returned to the verandah.

"Poor Jack," he murmured, referring to their former groomsman, "you know he was always cash-strapped, and tried to make a living as a professional wrestler. However carefully choreographed the actions in the ring are, they're made to look as injurious as possible, consistent of course with survival to stage the next bout, and so accidents can happen, but they're seldom as grievous as the one I've just been told about."

"What has happened?" Helene asked, her hand up to her mouth.

"Jack was thrown against the edge of the ring, neck first. He's in hospital, speechless and paralysed."

She could not reply, for she had to hurry down to the churchyard to rescue one of her children, who was wailing bitterly after tripping and knocking his face, fortunately not very hard, against a gravestone.

A ring at the doorbell signalled the arrival of the minister of the church. "The floor," he explained, when Helene's cup of tea and slices of banana cake were placed before him, "was rotten, beetles and damp, you know, and had to be replaced. It took some years and several cunningly pointed sermons to wring the necessary funds out of the parishioners. Underneath, the workmen found this." He handed her a ring, which she passed to her husband.

"But this," he said, turning it over and over, "is a brass curtain ring!"

"I was there when it was found, and can vouch for the fact that there was nothing else of value under the floor." The husband and wife looked at each other in bewilderment, while the minister's wry smile and beady-eyed stare appraised their reaction. He evidently expected them to blush with embarrassment at being reminded how they couldn't or wouldn't afford a decent wedding ring.

Before he died, however, the erstwhile groomsman and wrestler recovered sufficiently to be able to dictate a death-bed confession. He had indeed stolen and pawned the gold wedding ring, being, as he put it, "perennially short," and staged a clumsy pretence of losing it at the very moment when it was most needed. Strength failed him before he could say what had become of it after that.

But surely someone would like to say. The space below is intended for any reader who wishes to supply a suitable dénouement for the story, to round it off as it were, always bearing in mind the size of the space available, and the advice Polonius gave but didn't heed himself, that brevity is the soul of wit.

The present author will only add this. The green patch where the children had fallen down was dug up to receive the wrestler's coffin, a sign of an enlightened age's dismissal of superstitions regarding what would happen to anyone who disturbed a fairy ring. But Helene was almost sure that, looking out of her window late one Midsummer's Eve, she saw a band of little folk dancing vigorously around the grave, and in the midst of them a tall figure built like a wrestler leaping back and forth in a vain effort to catch a looping gold circlet they were flinging from one to another.

15

The Cave on the Mountain

It being school holidays, Fiona and her twin brother Joseph went exploring up the mountain whose lower slopes abutted on the house where they lived. Joseph kept their pocket money, for he had pockets and a purse, to spend at the restaurant on their way down. Short-cutting at first the zig-zags on the path up the steep hillside, and then glad enough to follow them, they reached at last the belt of trees where the contour path began, under the rocky cliffs that towered up to the unassailable peak. Some way along they branched off up a narrow gully, dank with seeping water and wet fronds of maidenhair that swished

against their thighs, and gloomily overhung with leafy branches, where birds twittered and strange beasts scuttled.

"It's too steep, and frightening," panted Fiona. "I'm going back."

"Look," said Joseph, his hand on the rocky wall at one side of the gully. "Behind that bush, there's a cave!"

"I'm not going in there. Toads live there!"

"What's wrong with toads? They're not leopards or hyenas!"

"They're slimy and horrible," said Fiona, following him in nevertheless. They had to bend their heads under the low roof. It was not very deep, but sloped upwards. The floor was stony and wet, littered with dead leaves and animal droppings that gave it a rank, pungent smell. As their eyes got used to the gloom they made out an empty wine bottle in a corner, and a ragged, rotting blanket on the driest part of the floor.

"Look what somebody's left!" exclaimed Joseph with distaste. "And broken sandshoes all full of holes underneath! Do you think anybody ever slept here?"

"Best house when it rains," said a deep voice, and the stooping bulk of a large ragged man filled the doorway. The children shrank back with a little cry of alarm.

"We're just going, sir," said Joseph nervously.

"Sit down!" Terrified, they subsided, though there was nowhere comfortable to sit.

A big hand reached towards Joseph's pocket. "Money!" the caveman demanded.

"We've only this," stammered Joseph, as the purse was snatched out of his hand. "We always buy an iced orange drink at the restaurant on the way down."

"Not today! What have you got?" he asked Fiona.

"N- nothing!" she stuttered. He stared at her, his eyes gleaming hungrily as if he would like to swallow her, and pointed at her neck. "Chain!" he said.

"My—my locket? It's my birthday present."

"Give!"

She shrank back, eyes wide with fear, while impatiently he reached forward and tore it off. He ignored her cry of pain, and looked meaningfully at Joseph's shoes. His own feet were wound in rags.

"Mine will never fit you, sir," Joseph pleaded.

"Bring shoes. Big shoes!" the man insisted.

"Where—how—?"

"We'll bring them, tomorrow, promise!" cried Fiona desperately.

"Otherwise wring necks like chickens!" the man threatened, and sobbing the children crawled past him and ran down the gully as fast as the dangerously uneven terrain permitted.

Reluctance struggled with obedience for fear of unknown consequences, in Joseph's palpitating breast. In the end the oppressive authority of the adult world proved too much to ignore. The only shoes he could possibly take to the mountain man were his father's. He was wearing his work shoes, so the pair Joseph took out of the wardrobe next morning were new ones. The nicer they were, he thought, the less chance there was that his neck would be wrung like a chicken's.

Fiona was afraid to go, Joseph afraid not to. The cave, to his relief, was empty. He placed the shoes on the rotten blanket , with half a cake he had taken from the pantry, and hurriedly departed.

The children looked guiltily at each other as they heard the maidservant interrogated about the missing shoes and the purloined cake, which latter "she had only to ask for," but "the shoes had to be found." They weren't, of course, and the children heard their parents discussing whether the girl should be dismissed. Then they had nightmares about the caveman, and woke screaming, and when comforted Fiona blurted out the details of their adventure and its aftermath.

"Show me the cave!" their father ordered, and Joseph reluctantly at first, but soon enjoying the rare felicity of a mountain hike with his father, did so. "Perhaps we'll catch sight of the tramp who robbed you, and then I'll have something to say to him!" growled his father.

"I don't think he was a really bad man," Joseph ventured. "He hasn't a very nice house." But his father was not appeased.

There was no sign of the tramp. The shoes were still where Joseph had left them, but spoilt by damp and dirt and sadly damaged by the teeth of whatever rodents had devoured the cake and shredded its container.

"He's not been back. He never believed you'd be so foolish as to bring a pair of brand new shoes!" his father expostulated. "Look at them! Good for nothing now!"

"Underneath they're still good," the boy muttered.

"Come out of this stinking cave, and don't you ever go into these lonely places again!" Angrily his father flung the gnawed and mutilated shoes across the gully and marched his crestfallen son away. Then he reproached himself for littering, but barked his shins on rocks and scratched his arms on thorns when he went back to look for them, and gave up the search in irritation.

"What on earth made you think you had to bring my shoes to that thieving scoundrel?" he asked crossly.

"He told me to," the boy replied. "He needed them."

Higher up the gully the tramp waited till the man and boy were safely far away before cautiously retrieving the discarded shoes. With his knife he prised open the uppers so that his toes could stick comfortably out, and then carefully adjusted the boy's innocent if misguided generosity over the rags on his feet.

16

Phoebe

Phoebe was about to undertake a long sea voyage. God would protect her, she said, and if the captain and sailors were willing to risk the winds and the waves, she would be at least as safe as they. A matron who had lived all her life on the isthmus of Corinth, within sight of the sea, she had never yet ventured upon it. For many years she had helped fellow worshippers at the little house church her friend had established, and now he persuaded her she should see Rome also. He would compose a letter commending her to people he knew there.

The letter, a long one, was painstakingly written by a secretary from dictation, and notes compiled over a long period, because Phoebe's friend had bad eyes. The secretary brought it to her after she had fussily seen her luggage into the narrow cabin allocated to her. "You seem to have forgotten this," he said. "Look after it, for it's your only guarantee of a warm welcome!"

"Oh, I'll get by," she said, thrusting the little scroll carelessly into her bosom, "if I can manage with all these sailormen swarming about. There's hardly room to stretch, and if the ship rolls about like this in port, I don't know how we can be expected to keep our legs when we're on the open sea!"

Leg-keeping was not too difficult among the isles of Greece, once the pitch and roll of the ship had stopped making her feel nauseous, but when they veered westwards a sudden storm blew up. Shouting men rushed to pull down the sails, the ship dipped and plunged like an unbroken horse, then reared desperately up one mountainous wave after another, spun hither and thither, and seemed every moment about to be overwhelmed by the foam washing more and more fiercely over the listing deck.

Dashed against the rails and finding herself in an almost vertical position looking down into the sea, Phoebe saw her letter of introduction, which for some reason she had taken out of the cabin bag where she usually kept it, fly overboard, bob briefly on a scudding wave, and vanish from her sight.

"There is little point surviving now to be rejected in Rome," she thought. "I only pray that when I drown I may go as quickly as the little scroll I have lost!"

But somehow, much later it seemed, she found herself on the bunk bed in her empty cabin, and the sea as smooth as the proverbial millpond.

The captain entered. "Sea was quite lively yesterday," he said. "Nasty experience for you, but you look much better now. Unfortunately we had to jettison most of the cargo, and I'm afraid that included your cabin bag. We have got one thing of yours, however, though not much use now. It was strangely washed up out of the sea on a wave that broke right over my head and almost took me away with it like Jonah!"

He handed her a partly dried but sadly limp and soggy scroll, the ink smudged, and she feared barely if at all legible.

"It's no good now," she said, so dispirited that she only wanted the voyage over, whatever its outcome. "Throw it overboard, and land me anywhere, the sooner the better. I shall never put to sea again!"

The captain snorted, took the scroll, and departed.

"Where are we?" Phoebe asked, when at last everyone was able to disembark. "Can this be Rome? Where are the seven hills I've heard about? But it doesn't matter. I know no one, and have nowhere to go and nothing to take with me."

"Rome is far inland," said the captain. "We will hire a conveyance and take you there. That, I'm sorry to say, is all we can do for you."

Arrived in Rome, the sailors dispersed, and the captain was the last to leave her. "Here," he said, "is part of your passage money. It will at least help you to find a night's lodging somewhere. And I didn't throw your scroll overboard. Take it. Who knows?"

Helplessly she started to walk up the street in front of her, meaning to ask some passer by the way to the nearest hostel. She allowed several to hurry past before she plucked up courage to accost an anxious-looking man she saw approaching. He cut her short as she began to explain she was a stranger just arrived from Corinth.

"Phoebe?" he said, to her amazement. "We heard you were coming, but understood that your ship was wrecked in the storm off Sicily. Come, the best lodgings we could procure are still ready for you! We have heard of your usefulness, and the help you have been to so many, and to Paul especially! You have his letter, I trust?"

"His letter?" she said in bewilderment, as he ushered her towards an imposing house nearby.

"We heard he had sent us a treatise, a profound exposition of divine doctrine—"

"It was soaked in the storm," she explained, passing him the bedraggled scroll. "I doubt if it can be read now. But it only bids you look after me, and you seem to be doing that wonderfully, even without what my friend may have said in it!"

"Oh, no," said the man, holding the scroll reverently in his hands and almost weeping as he gazed at it. "Paul's letter to the Romans says much more than that. We will read it, never fear!"

He smiled at her with a kindness greater than she could account for. " 'How beautiful on the mountains, or the sea, are the feet of him—of her—who brings glad tidings!' You have never been so useful, or so helpful, to Christians anywhere, born or yet unborn, as you have been now, safely delivering this letter to us!"

17

Outside Buckingham Palace

"**B**uckingham Palace, *ja*?" Count von Reichmeyer asked, as the taxi slewed round the crescent between the Albert Memorial and the Palace gates. "The guards will open the gates for us?"

"No," Wigglesworth told him shortly.

"No? *Nein*? You will signal? Give orders?"

Wigglesworth gazed at him in surprise. Was he still as naïve as when they had cannoned into each other during the football match while the shelling paused in France?

Von Reichmeyer, a fresh-faced boy of nineteen, was underneath him in the muddy hole into which they had fallen. He

smiled nervously as Wigglesworth, laughing, seized his hand to pull him upright. "Wigglesworth," he said.

"Von Reichmeyer."

"Merry Christmas."

"*Danke schön.*"

Soon after, the officers stopped the frivolities, and next morning Wigglesworth's company with fixed bayonets went over the top. Crawling past barbed wire fences, charging towards the enemy trenches, trying not to hesitate when men twisted and fell beside him, Wigglesworth dived flat as a shell screamed overhead. As it exploded behind him, showering him with soil and mud, he half rose, leapt forward, and found himself in a bunker with his bayonet levelled at the chest of a fresh-faced boy who gradually raised his hands, and then, recognizing his captor, smiled.

It was von Reichmeyer.

Managing to restrain the urge, born of fear as much as of training, to plunge his blade through the enemy's breastbone, Wigglesworth slowly lowered his rifle, and jerked his head in the direction he intended his prisoner to go. But suddenly he saw a flash and felt a searing pain in his side, and found von Reichmeyer on top of him, a pistol he had somehow produced pointing at his face. He could not believe his folly, the boy's adroitness, or the cunning betrayal of all the decencies of civilized behaviour that had duped him.

"One game I lose, this I win!" von Reichmeyer said, with another smile, triumphant this time, and Wigglesworth, no longer attacking, was forced to drag himself, wounded and bleeding, to the German lines. From there he was sent eventually to a castle on the Rhine, now used as a prisoner of war camp. "*Meine Schloß*, your prison," von Reichmeyer told him smugly, as the rail-car bore him away. There, hungry, wretched, ill-used and most of the time mind-numbingly bored, he sat out the years till the armistice freed him.

Returning home, to the narrow terraced house in a dirty and gloomy street in London's East End, he was received with surprise rather than delight. They had thought him dead long since; now he was another mouth to feed, when what work there was to be had, paid starvation wages. Jenny, the girl he had hoped to marry, had married someone else. Life without responsibilities in the more ample surroundings of the *Schloß* seemed almost preferable. Nevertheless, he cursed the wasted years, and above all the cunning deceiver whom he had had at his mercy and had allowed to get the better of him. Of *him*! He shuddered as he thought of the indignities to which that capitulation, to such a person, had subjected him.

He found employment as a sort of batman to his former commanding officer, himself an adjunct to a politician, and his prospects, financially and socially speaking, improved, but not the gnawing ache in his heart. Time and again he imagined a different outcome as he pointed his bayonet at the chest of a fresh-faced boy who slowly raised empty hands and smiled back at him.

Some years later his commander, or employer, a colonel now though hostilities were in abeyance, was deputed to meet a German ambassador, and Wigglesworth was given the task of looking after a member of his entourage. They met in an officers' mess, and it was von Reichmeyer who rose from the table when they approached.

Wigglesworth froze, but von Reichmeyer's face, less boyish now but as confident as ever, broke into a broad smile of recognition. "To this man, I owe my life!" he exclaimed. "He did not kill me! Instead, I too, saved his life."

"Saved it? You smothered it!" Wigglesworth burst out. Surely he would not be required to be of service to *him*, of all people?

"*Englanders!*" said von Reichmeyer with a shrug. "*In meine Schloß* he lived safely for the whole war. Who knows what death, gassing, maiming he might have suffered from the bullets and the barrage in those muddy fields where we played—*ach!*—football?"

"Do you call that cold and dreary prison *your 'Schloß'*?" Wigglesworth asked scornfully.

"Indeed, it is my home, where I was born. I am Count von Reichmeyer. And you, where do you live?"

"Buckingham Palace!" Wigglesworth snorted, witheringly.

"So? You will show me London, *ja*?"

There was no help for it. The colonel had a taxi ready for them. They were to cruise round for an hour or so, and then meet the ambassador's party outside the Houses of Parliament. Seated next to his former foe, Wigglesworth had a vision of a pistol appearing unexpectedly in a cowed and beaten hand; this time, however, with a sudden and skilful twist of the wrist, he would triumphantly disarm his opportunistic adversary. He was in London, after all, cruising beside the Thames, not the Rhine. But how could he hate this cheerful man, so confidently assured that he had in fact saved rather than destroyed him?

"It is illegal to stop here," he told his companion outside the gates of the Palace.

"Illegal, for *you*?"

"For any vehicle."

"But—" Again that naïve frown of perplexity, that boyish bewilderment Wigglesworth suddenly remembered as he lay atop of the fallen footballer.

"It is true that I am no more than a Count you did not kill, and that we did not win the war. But I showed you hospitality in my own house for years, and yet you refuse to have me one afternoon to enter your palace, Herr Prince?"

18

The Giant's Shoe

The shoe was really a half boot, for one end of it would have covered the ankle. It sat alone on a patch of ground at the edge of a not very thriving housing estate, but not forlornly, for there was always smoke ascending from the chimney in the roof that capped the tall bit where the leg would have gone. It didn't look like many a lost shoe, for it had been carefully converted into a dwelling for the old woman, actually not so old, and the twenty-four orphans she had managed to cram into the round toe-end of it. Twelve boys slept in the large end room, which had an emergency door into the playground outside, and six girls in each of the two rooms next to it. The

main door was on the other side in the ankle end of the shoe, and led into the kitchen quarters, which had a storeroom above. That wasn't the best place for the stores, perhaps, since hot air rises; it should have been the old woman's bedroom, but she preferred to sleep in what had originally been intended as the storeroom, to be nearer her charges, who often needed comforting or disciplining, although the older ones were supposed to help her care for the younger ones as much as possible. There was a big bathroom between her and the children, so that she didn't find the noise they sometimes made too deafening. She had a kind word for everyone, and a strap for some, that she didn't often have to use.

You'll notice there was no separate recreation room, but on wet days they would push the beds aside in the big end room for games or reading. She taught them all to read, and had a bookcase full of books which they were encouraged to use; in fact, the older ones were required to spend a certain time every day reading to the younger ones, till they were old enough to read for themselves.

The shopping and the cooking the old woman mostly did herself, but she would take some children down to the shops to help carry home the parcels; this she let them think a special privilege, and hoped the chaos would not be worse than usual when they returned. Then they would help her peel potatoes and vegetables, and prepare meat, when there was any. At mealtimes the children crowded very closely around the kitchen table, where occasionally, but not too often, I'm afraid, there was pudding to be enjoyed. The old woman always carefully said grace before they "fell to with an appetite."

But then one dark, cloudy morning the giant came for his shoe. He made a great noise about it, stomping through the fields and woodlands round about, and clattering over the streets of the housing estate, before he found what he wanted.

Then he broke off the chimney, tore away the roof from the ankle end of the shoe, turned the whole thing upside down, and tapped out the contents on the ground.

Of course, the old woman had heard the giant coming, and as soon as he started wrenching at the chimney made sure that everyone tumbled out. They used both doors and in a few cases a window or two, while all the furniture landed in broken heaps in the midst of them. But when she managed to gather all the terrified children together in a safe place, she could only count twenty-three, and this took some time, because some wouldn't keep still and got counted twice.

Meanwhile the giant was fitting his great foot into the shoe. "Wait!" she screamed, running forward and falling flat in the wind his movements were making. "Jack's still in there!"

The shoe seemed to be waving in the air, but before it disappeared entirely, out tumbled Jack, and everyone cheered, for he was a helpful and popular boy. He landed in a heap, but jumped up immediately, and crawled and ran helter-skelter to the safe place where the others were huddling. When the giant went away, and everyone stopped feeling frightened and began to think it had all been rather exciting, they burst out singing because although their home was gone nobody had been injured.

"We shall have to rehouse them somewhere," the city fathers said when the damage was investigated. "She deserves commendation for taking the poor orphans off the streets. The condemned building we refurbished for them to live in was never really adequate for the numbers she insisted on looking after. There will be other claims, for injuries and houses damaged in the hurricane that were not properly insured, but meanwhile they must be accommodated in the Town Hall."

When the children were asked their version of what had happened, they described the giant's careless cruelty in awestruck and vivid terms.

"It wasn't really a giant, you know," said the chairman of the city fathers, who disapproved of the over-imaginative sort of teaching the old woman seemed to have been giving them.

"Oh, it was," said a little girl named Jemima. "We heard him coming and saw what he did!"

"Then where did he go?"

"Why, up the beanstalk, of course!"

"I don't see any beanstalk," the city father said, with a frown.

"That's because Jack chopped it down!" Jemima answered, clapping her hands. "Didn't you, Jack?"

"Not exactly *chopped*," Jack admitted.

"It's lying there," Jemima insisted, "with a great big hole at the end, which the giant made when he fell all the way down!"

She drew the city father towards the woodland to see. A huge tree that had towered above the skyline at one end of the field had been uprooted, and stretched all the way across the road and beyond. Its exposed roots had lifted a great mass of soil out of the ground, leaving a gaping hole which Jemima was convinced the giant had made in his tremendous fall.

19

Skating for Glory

To gasps of admiration from the crowd, Monica, with one leg raised directly above the other and her nose practically touching the skate on the ice, skimmed away from her successful triple jump. Then, effortlessly, she pirouetted and spun like a top before ending with an elegant motionless curtsey. As she floated off waving, to rapturous applause, Frederick her coach and lover stood up and shouted, "Ten, at least!"

But the judges awarded only nine, because of some hitch in the performance apparent only to them. And then out whizzed little Angela, light and pretty as a fairy, athletic as a

young roe on the mountain tops, and did all that Monica had done, with a frolicsome ease that earned her the prize.

"She was good," Frederick admitted, as he drove Monica home, "but not *that* good!"

"I can beat her," Monica promised. "A somersault would beat her. She'd not risk that!"

"Neither must you. It's not permitted, anyway. You might crack your skull on the ice, and I'd rather your brains stayed in that lovely head of yours!" Then, while she simpered, he bobbed a kiss at her cheek, although he was driving.

The date for the country's championships was approaching, and it was clear that Monica and Angela were the only serious candidates for the victor's accolade.

Angela was walking with her skates over her shoulder by the side of the canal on the way to the practice rink. Driving up the road behind her, Frederick playfully said, "If I side-swipe her into the canal, you'll win hands down!" Then he revved the engine to make the car jump forward.

"Frederick!" Monica screamed, believing he seriously meant to injure her rival, and in a moment of panic seized the wheel. The car swerved sideways, skidded off the verge and crumpled against a tree. The passenger door flew open, and Monica was thrown out, narrowly missing the tree in her flight.

She rose gingerly as a crowd gathered, and Frederick extricated himself from the wreckage as anxiously and angrily as shock permitted to see what had become of her.

"I'm all right," she said, wincing as she put her foot to the ground.

"Will you be fit for the contest?" Angela asked anxiously. "It won't be any fun without you!"

"Fun!" snorted Frederick. To him it was war.

"I'll skate if I have to do it from a wheelchair!" Monica promised.

The only serious injury was to the car. It was some appreciable time before Frederick could afford to replace it, in spite of insurance. When the day of the championship arrived Monica assured him that she was as fit as ever. And indeed when it was her turn on the ice she skated with a rhythmic fluency that belied the fears caused by the accident. But to Frederick's mortification, when the point in her routine arrived where she was wont to execute her thrilling triple jump, she did not attempt it. She finished to considerable applause, but the judges rightly awarded her insufficient marks to beat Angela.

So it was Angela who made national headlines, and flew to Europe to skate for the honour of being crowned world champion.

"How could you have been so *stupid*?" Frederick berated his protégé bitterly. "You could have been champion! Now—"

Monica bit her lip. It was not only his car, but his pride and her career she had ruined.

She loved skating too much to abandon it. Freed from the stress of competition, she glided about the rink simply for the joy of it. Once, on a public day, she was not recognized until she started to execute intricate manoeuvres among the more pedestrian skaters, and then voices began to murmur, "It's Monica Birnbaum!"

Frederick proudly told announcers she might give an exhibition if the ice were cleared.

To her surprise and momentary confusion, she heard a loudspeaker announce, "Ladies and gentlemen, we have the rare privilege of seeing a future world champion in action among us! Please give Miss Birnbaum five minutes alone on the ice so that we can enjoy an exhibition of her skills. I understand from her manager and coach Mr Frederick Gainsworth (applause, please!) that she has kindly consented..."

"Oh, have I?" thought Monica. But ushers were clearing the ice, even of the few plodders who objected, and as she began her initial movements zest for her chosen sport took possession of her.

"Look at that!" cried Frederick, as she flew across the ice, dancing, pirouetting, spinning. "She's really going for it! Bravo, Monica, bravo!" He stood up, applauding vigorously.

She paused at one end of the rink, then like a stormy petrel picking up speed flew faster than ever, almost as far as the other end. "The triple jump! She means to do it!" Frederick exclaimed. Into the air she leapt, spun, once, twice, was there room enough for a third? Oh yes, and landing, down she crouched on one knee, the knee of the leg she had twisted in the accident. She circled safely and rose, though she felt a needle-like twinge as the muscle twitched under the pressure. But people were clapping, and once again the heady sound of cheering was ringing in her ears.

She did not finish with the routine Frederick expected. Her leg was objecting to further punishment, but her determination did not falter. Gritting her teeth she skated forward, faster and faster.

"What is she doing now?" Frederick asked in surprise. "Surely—no, no, she mustn't!" He leapt up, shouting, "No, Monica, don't think it!"

But the bit was between her teeth. This time she would soar, up, up and over, looping, like a Catherine wheel. What a pity she had not lights on her costume in a darkened amphitheatre!

Faster she went, faster than ever, and then up, back-flipping till she was almost vertical, and jack-knifing over …

"Monica!" Frederick yelled, the only sound in a momentarily silent arena.

20

The Cat on the Stair

It was so gloomy at the top of the stairs that the cat was almost invisible; only its glowing green eyes caught Bill Jones's attention, and he paused in surprise, for he was sure the house he had rented contained no cat. By the time he had mounted the stair it had slunk away, and he could not find it, but he put out a saucer of milk. Next morning, however, the offering remained untouched, and the cat did not return.

In the eighteenth century the house had stood in large grounds in an isolated village; now it hid behind old trees in an unkempt garden at the end of a narrow alley in a built-up area. It was too large for Jones's needs, but conveniently close

to the newspaper offices where he worked. Odd relics of its past included a windowless cellar reached by a short staircase from the kitchen, perhaps for wine bottles or a kitchen maid; and a couple of attics for lumber or a butler and housekeeper.

Some old wainscot in the cellar had rotted in places, and poking about behind it Jones found a clumsy rag doll, with a pin through its heart. What grim reminder was it of an ill-used kitchen wench's impotent vindictiveness against a cruel mistress? He placed it on the mantelpiece in the living room, as a museum piece that deserved preservation.

At four one morning he was awakened by the cat jumping lightly on to the foot of his bed, but when he reached out to touch it, it seemed to have disappeared. It was at first silent, but some nights later he heard it purring, and soon after he was actually able to feel its fur. But it was always absent when he looked for it, and never tasted any of the food he put out.

One evening he heard sighing when he entered the house. It was a cold, wet night, and he put the sounds down to the wind in the chimney. On another occasion, however, he was almost convinced he could hear the muted sniffs and sobs of a child crying—the wind again, or some airlock in the water pipes, he concluded.

But then one night, as his eyes grew used to the gloom at the top of the stairs, what he thought was the cat merged into the dim outline of a young girl who seemed to be sitting there weeping. But when he spoke to her he found he was mistaken: the stairs were empty.

Another night, however, as he lay in bed, he distinctly heard an older woman calling, "Puss, puss, puss!" and the clink of a saucer on a wooden floor, followed by the unmistakable sound of a cat lapping milk. But by the time he had found the light switch there was no one there.

His next hallucination, as he thought it must be, was the woman's grey head motionless on his pillow, and a girl of about thirteen or fourteen, in servant's uniform, looking down at her with an awestruck expression.

The vision passed rapidly, but he could not refrain from leaving the bedroom in a hurry. This time he very nearly tripped over the cat, which meowed loudly and scratched his ankle. He missed his footing on the last stair or two, and landed full length on the carpet at the bottom. He lay shocked for some seconds, and saw the servant girl coming down the stairs towards him. Her mouth was working as if she was speaking, but he could not catch what she was saying. His ankle quivered where the cat had scratched it, his shoulder ached where he had fallen upon it, and suddenly a thrilling pain shot deep into his chest in the area where the doll had a pin through its heart.

The girl was talking urgently to him, but he could hear no sound. She was gesticulating towards the living room, and weeping as she did so. Through the door he could see the doll on the mantel shelf, and she seemed to be making movements like one pulling threads through the eye of a needle. Then he realized she was urging him to pull the pin out of the doll, the pin that seemed to be transfixing his own heart.

She was in the room trying to reach the doll, but unable to touch it. It was substantial, she was not.

Somehow he dragged himself to his feet, and staggered towards her, the pain increasing as he raised his hands to seize the doll. With an effort he managed to pull out the pin before he collapsed on the floor. A child's voice, distant but distinct, said, "Thank you! Oh, thank you!"

* * *

When Jones was well enough to delve into his newspaper's archives, he discovered a notice of the death of an old lady whose frightened servant girl admitted, at a subsequent trial, that she had brought it about by stabbing an effigy of her to the heart. "She beat me," she explained, "but I'm sorry, oh so sorry!" Asked to produce the effigy, she said she had lost it. "Then," said the judge, "we must assume you poisoned your mistress." Accordingly, she was condemned to death.

Searching further, Jones discovered that the unduly harsh sentence was commuted on appeal, after an impassioned plea by a philanthropic lawyer, who argued that no civilized court in an enlightened eighteenth century could justly condemn anyone, let alone a child, who confessed to murder by sympathetic magic, which only old wives and superstitious children could think effective. Moreover, a learned physician was present to attest that there was no evidence of poisoning.

The century was an age of sentiment as well as of enlightenment. A journalist recorded that the onlookers shed tears when the child kissed the hand of the lawyer who had pleaded for her, and sobbed, "Thank you! Oh, thank you!"

21

Mountain Goat Leap

Southern tourists in the Cascades were listening, more or less, to the guide, the attentive ones glad of a breather, the energetic ones impatient to reach the viewing platform. "Up there," she told them, "you can look down the valley and see the mountain goats on their way to drink at the pools."

Panting somewhat, for the mountain track was steep, they were almost at the summit of the wooded ridge when they found their way blocked by a splendidly polar-looking shaggy-haired Rocky Mountain goat that was straddling the path. It stared dumbly back at the entranced procession and

made no sign of budging. The guide, who was leading, retreated hastily.

"It looks docile enough," one woman said. "I'd be a bit afraid of brushing past it, so can't you shoo it away first?"

"I'm not that expendable," said the guide. "Did you see how I backed up? You might almost think you could walk up to him and pat him on the nose, but don't try it! That's a wild animal, and he'll have your heart out on the end of his horns before you can raise your hand!"

The tourists all took a pace or two backwards, and some of them swallowed hard. "Nobody wants a punctured lung," a medical student said knowingly.

Cameras flashed, until the goat, disturbed at last, trotted over the cliff edge with sure-footed agility and made its precarious way down into the valley. Then the tourists congregated on the viewing platform to exclaim delightedly at the magnificent scenery, and at a line of goats trooping down a steep incline, following a path they and their ancestors had beaten out over countless ages in the past.

"That," said the guide, pointing at the procession, and wishing to impress on the tourists the full significance of what they were seeing, "has been going on for thousands of years!"

"And they're not a bit tired!" someone quipped, grinning round for applause he didn't get. Somewhat mortified, he added, "They probably think we've been grandstanding them just as long!"

"They're more intelligent than you might expect," another tourist observed drily. "They've learnt to tolerate and on the whole ignore the silly humans who traipse all the way up here where they've no business to be, only to gawp and make wisecracks. Think of their history: undisturbed for aeons, until hunters came, and then no doubt prospectors, who at least had a purpose, now they're bothered by the greatest nuisance of all. Us!"

"And archaeologists," added the guide, pretending to ignore the observer's sarcasm. "They're looking for evidence of early human interference in the ecology of this part of the Cascades, and trying to ascertain if possible when the first migrations of mountain goats, which are actually a kind of antelope, into these regions took place."

"Diggers are sure to find what they think ought to be here," said the wisecracker, hoping to redeem himself, "and we'll have to believe whatever they tell us!"

"Fossil or other datable remains might show whether they spread south from the Yukon or north from the Rockies," the guide persisted patiently.

"South," said the sarcastic observer, "if they came over when Siberia was joined to Alaska."

"North," countered the wisecracker, "if they jumped the Atlantic when it was a narrow trench."

"I think God put them here, and that's all we need worry about," said the woman who had thought the mountain goat looked docile. "People shouldn't be allowed to dig up this beautiful mountain!"

"They pick only the likeliest spots and don't disturb more than they have to," explained the guide with a weary smile. "Actually, they've found evidence of some very early encampments: hearthstones, arrowheads of iron, and stone implements at a lower level, and even an inscription at a lower level still!"

"That's impossible!" exclaimed a sceptic. "Stone age people couldn't write."

"Perhaps they could," someone ventured mildly. "Aliens may have landed and taught them. Well, it's possible, don't you think?" she added defensively.

"No," laughed the guide. "The inscribed stone must have been buried by the first new American mountain man who got as far North-west as this. He was illiterate, so what he carved took experts ages to decipher, the archaeologist in charge told me."

"What did it say?" an eager chorus asked.

"Museum authorities eventually made out, 'Bill Stumps his mark'."

"Really?" several tourists asked in surprise.

"That's from *Pickwick*," remarked the sceptic. "He could hardly have been illiterate, if he'd read *Pickwick*."

"The archaeologist was convinced he couldn't read anyone, let alone Pickwick, whoever Pickwick was," the guide assured her puzzled audience, "for otherwise Bill Stumps would have put his signature, not just his mark!"

The silence while this reasoning was being digested was broken by the woman who had questioned whether the goats were aggressive. "Oh, look," she said, pointing down the valley. "There's a little kid bouncing along next to his mother. See how high it can spring! What a cute little creature! I wish its mother would take more care to see it doesn't fall and hurt itself on that steep cliff!"

"I guess the young kids often break their legs or crack open their skulls," the wisecracker suggested. "It's Nature's way of controlling the population."

"How can you be so horrible?" the woman cried. "Just look at the clever way the dear little thing is jumping and sliding down that stony path! Ooh, precious, do be careful!"

"Well," sighed the guide, "if you've seen all you want to, we had better be making our way down again. Be careful where you put your hooves—boots, I mean. We're none of us leaping goats!"

"Or kids," said the wisecracker, who had to have the last word. "We'll just have to stir our bill stumps as best we can!"

And down to their waiting bus the procession of hornless bipeds trooped.

22

Quantum Physics

The syringe-shaped swordfish that was fiercely intent on bayoneting Joe-John punctured the space-time continuum in which he floated so that he slipped through a worm hole into what seemed like a new solar system. In comparison to its immense size he was a mere quantum particle subject to such intense gravitational forces that he found himself in two places at once. Moving too fast to locate his position, and positioned too imprecisely to measure his speed, he was both somewhere and nowhere. Though one person, he suffered rather than enjoyed twin simultaneous experiences in discrete parts of a single atom of an organization whose nature and immensity were beyond conjecture.

Joe
found himself in a desert landscape of low flowerless bushes on the shore of a pre-Cambrian sea. From the sultry soup-like water crept an ancestral arthropod that extended knife-like claws toward him, its beady eyes fixed mesmerically upon his. He shrank back with a terrified scream. The claws hesitated and withdrew, but he still shuddered in agoraphobic horror at the creatureless waste behind him. How could he ever hope to escape from the undeveloped emptiness of the land into which he feared to flee and from the predatory life-forms of his ancestors that were emerging belligerently from the sea? He flailed wildly about until he found the air around him too thick and heavy to strive against, and subsided helplessly. The huge arthropod clattered over the shells and pebbles of the beach and stood menacingly over him. Squelching across the sand out of the softly bubbling surf came a slimy

John
who was the same as Joe but must be designated differently found himself on the seven thousandth floor of a hovering building, being probed by investigative devices that implacably invaded every secret corner of mind and body. "Still a disappointingly limited and simple construction," an alien intelligence implied rather than said of the latter, "and with a pathetically small range of interests and understanding," it added contemptuously of the former. "To think we are descended from this! There's little we could tell it that it would find useful, even if it were not in such a state of emotional instability that it is unlikely to be able to absorb any information we may contrive to give it." Angry and insulted, John shouted, "Give me my due if not my dignity: I'm a person, not an it!" This provoked the equivalent of an alien chuckle, and the words "Show him, then!" A kaleidoscope of whirling

mollusc that claimed the attention of the lobster-like crab in a prehistoric confrontation that was either meaningless or likely to prove fatal to one or both of them. The crab stretched open hideous mandibles and the snail raised its absorbent engulfing belly. Joe shut his eyes and waited for dissolution.

colours and dizzily spinning vast expanses of scenery seemed to be exploding in John's brain before his anguished cries for the experiment to be stopped were listened to, and he sank panting into a grey aura of silent misery from which he feared to awaken. But he had little hope that worse was not still in store for him.

"Perhaps," said the psychiatrist to his colleague, laying down his syringe, "we should lessen the dose, or withdraw the hypnotic drug entirely, for it seems to be increasing the aggressiveness of the patient rather than calming him, and is probably inducing the frightening hallucinations that must be agitating him. But I'm loth to release his restraints without first sedating him."

He looked down at his helpless patient and shook his head sadly. "Oh, what a noble mind is here o'erthrown," he quoted. "He was quite a famous nuclear physicist in his day—in his own narrow circle, of course."

"Biologist, wasn't he?" said his colleague carelessly.

"One or the other," the psychiatrist replied. "It doesn't matter. He's nothing much at all now."

"Oh, I am, I am," cried Joe, but his voice made no sound in the pre-Cambrian wasteland. The mollusc was sliding back into the sea, the crab digging its way into the sand.

"Take me back to where I belong," pleaded John.

"Shall we let him go?" enquired an alien intelligence. "We've seen all we need, and he's nowhere near ready for us. It would be a mere artificial survival for him here."

The psychiatrist and his colleague looked round in amazement as Joe-John sat up and enunciated clearly the slogan "E = mc^2," and then added quietly, "except on a quantum level!"

23

Two Amphorae

Alexandros the billionaire shipping magnate was celebrating his and his wife's wedding anniversary on board his luxury yacht. The two dozen or so celebrities (politicians, actors, pop-singers, footballers, with their spouses or partners) around the mahogany table in the main saloon raised their crystal glasses as their host proposed the toast.

"Dear friends," he said, "and my beautiful wife Lucilla, who gave up a scintillating Hollywood career to marry me"— Lucilla Glinton (born Lucy Gleek) had not had her contract renewed after her two terrible films had flopped—"the wine you are about to taste is the oldest in the world. It has been

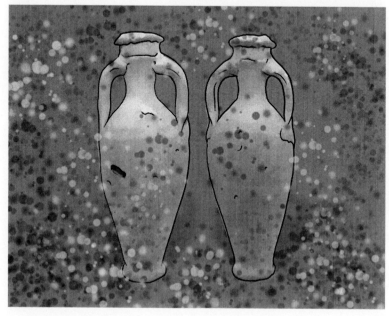

dredged up in one of two amphorae from the Mediterranean seabed where an ancient Athenian merchant vessel foundered two and a half millennia ago. The other, alas, was smashed, like, I fancy, the fishes who doubtless tasted its contents." (Laughter) "Its value, I need hardly say, like that of this yacht and our friendship, is inestimable! Its history, could we know it, might be no less interesting than I am sure its taste will prove to be. Let us therefore drink—"

At this point the photographer hired to record proceedings, having taken all the pictures he deemed necessary, retired, shutting the door behind him.

In ancient Athens Anaximenes was parting as amicably as circumstances permitted from his discarded wife. "It is not given to a mere woman to appreciate what a man undergoes when confronted by a twenty-year-old charmer as beautiful as Lupina," he told her. "Therefore, Seraphina, loving and desirable as you have been to me up to now, I have no choice but to follow her back to Rome. My house and vineyards you may henceforth consider your own. I ask only that in memory of our time together you send me at the next grape gathering a jar of your best vintage to grace my intended nuptials."

She smiled bleakly, and being a good submissive wife sensible of his kindness and consideration for her, promised to do as he requested. And in due course that is what she did.

However, painful though it is to record the fact, before the amphora containing the delectable beverage was tightly sealed, she visited an apothecary known for clandestine and illicit dealings with persons who paid him enough, and told him about polecats that were killing the chickens on her farm.

"I have the very thing for them, costly though it is," he replied, offering her a carefully packaged white powder. "The merest taste of this would shrivel up and consume Heracles himself more quickly than did the shirt of Nessus which his wife sent him! Therefore use it sparingly, cautiously, and wisely!"

She paid his exorbitant fee so readily that he wished he'd demanded double, and hurrying home tipped every last grain neither sparingly, cautiously, nor wisely into the wine she hoped her former husband and his new bride would drink at their wedding. Then she employed a merchant whose vessel was about to set sail for Rome to see it safely delivered to the villa where Anaximenes had told her they would be living.

But this same Anaximenes, who plied a liberal and lucrative trade between the ports of the Mediterranean, had poured many an oblation to Poseidon god of the sea, and consequently Poseidon felt more kindly disposed towards him than towards Seraphina. "It will amuse me," foamed the whimsical god, the white curls of his bearded surf breaking majestically about his blue-rollered head as he stirred up the necessary storm, "to frustrate her undutiful plan by swallowing her poisoned jar." Being immortal, he knew that it could not harm him.

Now the merchant, dissatisfied with the fee Seraphina had paid him, had contrived to smuggle on board, for his own use, a second amphora of wine from her well-stocked cellar. His ship therefore sailed for Rome with two of them stored side by side in the hold. But neither was destined to be broached before Poseidon's gleefully stirred up storm sent merchant and ship with all hands to the bottom.

And there, lost for aeons many fathoms down, the ship gradually disintegrated till only an anchor or two and some rotten spars remained, apart from the two amphorae, one intact, the other broken. These, divers using modern equipment were at last able to bring to the surface, and Alexandros paid a fortune to secure the sealed wine jar which he planned to open in memory of other nuptials than those for which one of the jars had originally been intended. But which of the two, the poisoned one or the one the merchant had stolen, had Alexandros bought? Had the apothecary's powder dissolved in the Mediterranean, or was it still waiting in lethal ambush for Alexandros, Lucilla and their guests to sample it?

The photographer, it will be remembered, had snapped the moment the guests were raising their ornate crystal glasses to lips no doubt tingling with delighted anticipation, and then had retired, closing the saloon door behind him. Photographs record only a single moment; little is to be inferred from them of what went before or came after. It pains us to confess that the only information available to us about the anniversary celebration is what the photographer provided.

You may have heard of Schrödinger's cat, famous because it can be proved to be both alive and dead. If a single photon of light that triggers a device that kills the cat is fired at it through a half-silvered mirror, the photon, being indivisible, both passes through the mirror and is deflected away by it, thus simultaneously both killing the cat and leaving it alive. Only when its current state is observed does it become either dead or alive. We may perhaps understand that light plying between the photographer's camera and its object acted in a similarly uncertain way, so that, since their fate can no longer be observed, Alexandros's guests must remain in a sort of narrative suspended animation.

24

Disasters at Canterbury

"**Y**ou need a new jacket," Charles's wife said. "Keep spruce, or they'll think I don't look after you properly."

"We can't afford it," he interjected hastily.

"I've bought it. You've got to make an impression before all those important professors at the conference. If you're going to get on, it's not what you know, it's who approves of you! The jacket fits perfectly: don't pretend it doesn't. It's the latest style, and the grey-brown checks are just eye-catching enough to be noticeable without shouting at anyone. Don't look like that: you can't be old-fashioned nowadays."

Charles smiled, and kissed her. "Thank you," he said. To him, a jacket was just a jacket.

He took the coach from London to Canterbury, accomplishing in an hour a journey that would have taken pilgrims in Chaucer's lifetime three days. Having established himself in his hotel room and hung his jacket in the cupboard, because the weather was hot, he visited a show illustrating Chaucer's *Canterbury Tales*. He found it amusing, especially the end, when the pilgrims reached a splendid mock-up of the Cathedral, which Chaucer's pilgrims never did, for his frame narrative stops short of the town, and which seemed a trifle absurd with the real thing just outside the door.

The conference included a guided tour of the Cathedral led by a local professor. One of the twin towers had been restored in the nineteenth century to look exactly like its medieval counterpart. "That one's genuine, the other's a fake," said the professor, waving in their general direction. Charles couldn't tell them apart, and soon forgot which was which.

Inside were the fifteenth-century decorations of the Lancastrian arms, and the tombs of the men who had precipitated the Wars of the Roses: Henry IV on one side, and on the other Edward the Black Prince whose son Henry had killed in order to seize the throne.

Then the delegates were shown the place where Thomas Becket was murdered, on 29th December 1170, accounting for Chaucer's twenty-nine pilgrims on the way to visit the shrine (no longer extant) of the martyred saint. It had stood between Henry and Edward, until iconoclasts destroyed it during the Reformation. To Charles, who unlike his medieval forebears did not expect help in times of sickness from the saint, a replica seemed pointless, turning a house of live spiritual worship into a museum of ancient atrocities.

Farther on, a row of tremendous pillars that soared up between splendid arches to support the roof was suddenly followed by a marked change in style. It was the reason for the alteration that Charles found most harrowing, after the political murders the guide had just described. The architect had fallen from the scaffolding and had had to be replaced by another who did not understand or did not care to follow his design. Charles imagined the scream as the poor man lost his footing on his precarious perch high up near the roof, and the terror of his fall to a painful death on the flagstones far below. What had his thoughts been as he plunged downwards? Of his present family, his unfulfilled future plans, the rash movement and momentary lapse in concentration that were about to cost him his life? It had all happened so long ago, but did that lessen the enormity of the disaster?

The days were so hot that Charles remained in his shirt-sleeves throughout the conference. Then he packed his bag and boarded the coach to return to London. He was nearly there, entering Lewisham, in fact, before he realized he was still in his shirtsleeves, and the jacket was still hanging in the cupboard where he had originally put it. Should he abandon it, new as it was?—but had not his wife laid out some of her own savings to purchase it so that he could cut a good figure at the conference? He felt guilty at not having worn it there. That fact he must keep to himself, but it was unthinkable that he should return home without it.

Had he time to retrieve it before it vanished for ever? Drawing a deep breath he dismounted in Lewisham, and, burdened by cumbersome luggage, waited impatiently for the next coach back to Canterbury. Would there even be another? He had almost decided to take a local bus home and face the music, when the coach arrived, and proved to be the last that was outward bound that afternoon.

"You're very lucky," the driver told him. "There's one seat left, because we had no show at the Elephant: someone who'd booked the journey didn't turn up. If they had, we wouldn't have stopped."

This time the coach seemed to amble; anxiously Charles counted the miles along the motorway that revealed little of the luxuriant Kentish countryside that pilgrims to Canterbury would have seen. The Cathedral no longer filled him with awe: the chance he might not find his jacket troubled him too much. As he entered the hotel, eyebrows rose at the sight of his return. He hurried to his room; the door stood wide open. But nobody had been in since he had left, and his precious jacket was still hanging in the cupboard.

"What happened?" a conference organizer asked him.

"I had to come back for my jacket," Charles said, grinning.

"How far had you got?"

"Lewisham!"

"What a *pain!*" the man commiserated with him.

An hour later the last coach that day left for London. While waiting for it Charles phoned his wife at a public kiosk.

"How did everything go?" she asked eagerly.

"Swimmingly," he replied cheerfully. "Excellent conference, wonderful city! The Cathedral's so magnificent it's all you can do not to fall on your knees! Mind you, it's full of disasters, but fortunately they're all historic!"

"And was your jacket a success?"

"Oh, yes. The weather's turned cooler than it has been, and I'm very glad I've got it. If you hadn't bought it for me I'd have been shivering now! What a disaster that would have been!"

25

Adoram the Tax Collector

A tax collector is seldom a popular figure, however faithfully and honestly he may perform what is after all only his duty. Adoram had been doing as he was told unwaveringly since the present King's grandfather's time. How respected and eagerly followed that King had been! His leather shield had checked many an arrow, his sword beaten down many an enemy weapon, the incredible accuracy of his sling-shot slain many an over-complacent foe. Thus he had established as a thriving kingdom a confederation of tribes that the follies of his half-mad predecessor had nearly brought to destruction. Now that he wanted to erect a centralized shrine

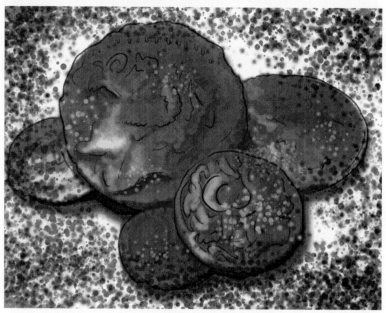

that would unite his people, they only half-reluctantly contributed to the demands levied in his name by the obedient Adoram.

His son succeeding him inherited a time of peace and the materials for the building that his father had collected. But he did not stop there. He practically turned the nation into a labour force who contributed much of their possessions as well as the sweat of their brows to the beautifying of the King's capital city. It might be said of him not that he found it brick and left it marble, but rather that however he found it he left it gold. Adoram realized that the burden on the people was becoming too great for them to bear. But he went on, as he was bidden, collecting the taxes required to feed the King's army of workmen and administrative officials and to build and embellish not only the golden shrine but palaces for innumerable foreign wives whom the King had married to cement alliances with potential enemies.

In due course this King died, and his young son was crowned and anointed in his place. Now the people of the tribes least associated with the one to which their King belonged elected a leader of their own who came with a deputation to the King requesting relief .

"What reply," the indignant King asked his councillors, "do they deserve for the effrontery of this attempt to escape their obligations?"

Never one to gainsay a superior, let alone the King, however foolish a youngster he might be, Adoram, loyal to his own detriment, could only frown gloomily, for he knew he would have to bear the initial brunt of the disgruntled populace's reaction. At least the experienced councillors, who had served the present King's father and in some cases his grandfather, advised caution, but the King's demeanour showed he was not likely to listen to their advice.

"Caution? Am I not King?" he answered angrily. "Wait till I have consulted those more in tune with the wellbeing of my kingdom than you people-placators!"

The young men he consulted had inherited luxuries from parents who had thrived in the time of the late King's affluence, and had no desire to relinquish what they believed they should enjoy in perpetuity; rather, they wanted their privileges increased now that their young contemporary was King.

Accordingly he summoned the representatives of the disaffected tribes and told them his little finger would be thicker than his father's loins: "My father chastized you with whips, but I shall chastize you with scorpions!"

Then an inventory was drawn of all the corn and wine and oil, the sheep and cattle and silver and gold that Adoram was to demand to satisfy the gluttony and avarice of the King's cronies and the huge court, made up of his closest tribesfolk, over which he presided.

"If you demand this of those hard-pressed tribesmen," Adoram's close friend Shemaiah warned him, "you will put yourself at risk! They have been galled too painfully for too long to respond with only sullenness and grumbling!"

"I know," Adoram answered, "but I shall have my enforcers with me, and the King must be obeyed."

"But will he be? That leader of theirs was so much his father's enemy that he had to flee to a far country because the King had ordered his death."

"Obeyed by me, I meant," replied Adoram mildly, "whatever the objections the surly people and their leader may make."

"Would it not be more sensible for you to refuse?"

Adoram laughed scornfully. "And be whipped by the King's scorpions? One death is as bitter as another. But I am not the

King's enemy. I served his father and his grandfather, and I shall serve him just as faithfully."

"They were not foolish as he is."

"Perhaps I shall prove that to him, and he will learn wisdom as a result."

Then steadily and resolutely, at the head of a small retinue of officials armed with staves, Adoram went down to the opposing camp and delivered the King's commandments.

An angry rumble, like the roll of approaching thunder, greeted Adoram's speech, increasing as he proceeded, until his words were drowned out. The officials supporting him, realizing their danger, at first shifted uneasily, then turned and fled. Adoram was left facing the people alone. The first stone that struck him made him stagger, but he did not turn. Instead he raised his hand and tried to shout above the rising clamour. Soon, however, a rain of missiles beat him down, and the bloodlust of the incensed mob was whetted rather than slaked on the helpless body of their victim.

From an eminence some way away, the King watched in disbelief as Adoram's retinue returned in disorder without their leader. "Have they dared to reject my demands?" he cried.

"Indeed, and will dare more," Shemaiah replied. "I warned him of his danger, but he hoped his example of compliance would encourage you to be more compassionate. Your wisest course now is first to flee and then to compromise."

"I shall retire with dignity and return with fire and slaughter."

"Then," said Shemaiah, "the entire kingdom will be destroyed."

But fortunately the King's tribesmen, more cautious or less loyal than Adoram, heeded the wisdom of Shemaiah rather than the folly of the King.

26

Shakespeare's Last Sonnet

"**H**e is hardly past fifty," the actors stormed, "and is he to waste his genius in luxurious retirement? We have had little or nothing from him for years!"

"Softly," said Judith. "He is ill!"

"He cannot be so ill that you can't persuade him to send us another *Twelfth Night* or *Lear* or *Tempest* to study and produce! Two plays a year that out-performed every playwright who ever presumed to entertain the city must mean he could still provide more if only he would bestir himself. He mustn't be allowed to become 'duller than the fat

weed that rots itself in ease on Lethe wharf!' Think of the rewards!"

"We have no more need of them," Susanna explained. The house at Stratford which the playwright's former colleagues had invaded was opulent enough. The frequent perilous and uncomfortable journeys he had had to make back and forth to the source of his wealth in London, to which he had never desired to relocate his family, were no longer necessary.

"But what of *our* dwindling incomes?" the actors cried. "The citizens have seen his plays, and want new ones. Revivals are losing their appeal, and today's wonders are tomorrow's yawns: no one writes as he has been doing for twenty years, and will he now bury a talent whose value increases with every investment it makes?"

"He has outpaced the University wits he once had to vie with," said Susanna. "He has no reason to strive any more."

"He believes that his poems will secure his fame for all time to come," said Judith simply. "His plays were patched up affairs that had their day upon the stage, and are mostly gone with the breath of the actors who performed them."

"His poems are struggles for the learned, his plays touch everybody. Without them his fame will dissolve with his bones in the church," said the actors sceptically. "He *must* write more, and we are here to see that he does!"

And they bustled into the sick man's bedroom and bullied him and his family, threatening to denounce them to the political authorities as dangerous Catholic sympathizers if he failed to continue supplying them with actable plays. Then and there they thrust pen and paper into his trembling hands and bade him get started, for his own, for his family's, for their and their audience's sakes, or there would be consequences. "What they are I know not yet, but they shall be the terrors of the earth!" one of them quoted significantly.

So the dying man dipped his quill into the proffered ink and wrote:

Constrained I am to summon back my Muse
Who may not heed my earnest pleas to come,
Which importunity should she refuse
My dearest loved ones face some fearful doom.
The tree that fears the feller's fell approach
Twice feels a biting axe attack his base,
But emptied casks are useless things to broach
Whose age-clogg'd spigot will not run apace.
Last scripts, tost off too lightly to deserve
The permanence of printed form, as mist
At sun-warmed morning fades no purpose serve
To make dull Night's advancing cloke desist.
    But might this sputtering quill spill one play more
    It would out-*Titus* all with these fools' gore!

Then the quill fell, scattering blots across the painfully scrawled lines, and the writer's brows drew down and his eyes closed. Susanna and Judith hurried to his side and seized his hands, but the bystanders eagerly snatched up the paper he had relinquished and read his final lines. Then disappointedly they looked from it to the pallid skin of the motionless head on the pillow, and stole quietly out of the room.

The sonnet was not included in Heminges and Condell's posthumous edition of the author's works, perhaps because they were unable to decide whether to include the vitriolic final couplet or to prefer the milder alternative offered as a possible substitute:

Of fame and wealth this life may have enough;
The next will give more glorious, richer stuff.

Had they done so, there would have been "much throwing about of brains" in learned journals and University departments, discussing the relative merits of the alternative endings, one seemingly more suited to the argument of the sonnet and the other to the situation of the patient, one suggesting his composure as death approached, the other irritation with the actors who had disturbed his comfort.

The manuscript was unsigned, and the poem, being unlikely to enhance either his reputation or that of the actors who had forced him to write it, was soon ignored and ceased to be circulated, so that it was not long before people forgot who its true author had been. What was remembered instead was the curse inscribed above his tomb in the parish church on any who should presume to remove his bones, possibly written to ensure that he would not be exhumed and reburied next to the woman a boyish indiscretion had forced him to marry, and if so, far more damaging to his reputation than a last sonnet like the one salvaged here would have been. She was after all the mother of children he loved and for whose support and enhancement all his exceptional works were written.

27

A Twoyill Scoodr

Nick adjusted the Santa Claus beard which a tug from his last customer had pulled awry, and seating the next little boy on his red-trousered knee asked him his name.

"Eddie."

Prickly sweat under the ruff at the back of his neck trickled itchily down his spine as Nick asked the regulation question, "What would you like for Christmas?"

"A twoyill scoodr."

He glanced enquiringly at the boy's father, who slightly shook his head. Either he was as mystified by the request as Santa himself, or he couldn't afford the gift, whatever it was.

"I'm afraid the elves aren't making those this year," Nick ventured.

"Oh yes," said the boy, pointing at the rows of scooters displayed nearby. "They've made lots, and I want one. James has one."

"Who's James?" Nick asked.

"A nasty boy at my school. He's got lots of toys."

As he dragged Eddie off, his father grunted glumly, "He'll be lucky if he gets a plastic ball!" and departed, shaking his head over the inequity of the capitalist system.

Nick's next customer was a little girl with chubby cheeks and a sticky mouth.

"What's your name, Sweetie?"

"Tweetie."

"Oh, Tweetie, is it? And what—"

"She means she wants a treat," her mother simpered. "A tweetie, she calls it. Her wants don't go beyond ice cream and chocolate marshmallows at present."

"Ask Father Christmas for a lovely dolly, Belinda," the next mother said, urging her little daughter forward.

"I don't want a doll. I hate dolls!"

"But why?" asked her distressed mother.

"They're girlie things."

"But you're a—"

"What *would* you like, Belinda?" Nick asked.

The child marched up to him and placing her tiny fists belligerently on his knees demanded, "Why do you have a brown beard under your white one?"

"Well, that one is growing, and this one isn't."

"Is it a fake, then," she asked pointedly, "a *real* fake?"

Yes, and so am I, thought Nick. I'm a mathematics student in a bedsitter trying to make some pocket money while my parents are paying for a course I'm not much good at.

Walking home that evening Nick recognized Eddie and his father as they turned in at a cottage to which Santa might be planning the delivery of a plastic ball. If he were a multi-millionaire, Nick fantasized, Eddie should have his scoodr, Tweetie her three-tier melba ice cream with a chocolate log poking up through the nut-clustered top, Belinda perhaps a space-gun to repel aliens or bearded zombies—but James should have nothing at all.

His stint in the heavy red costume ended late on Christmas Eve. Too tired to enjoy the prospect of a lonely Christmas, he plodded home past the twinkling lights of Christmas trees in the windows of the decorated houses, and past the façade of a great house lit up like an ocean liner at night, one that could only belong to the parents of such as the over-indulged James. For visible in the middle of sweeping lawns lay a red twoyill scoodr carelessly discarded on its side, the two wheels motionless and pathetically left to rust, but nonetheless ready to spin in response to the sweeping leg of an eager rider. A rider such as Eddie.

"I'm not a millionaire, but I can still be Saint Nicholas!" Nick said, and seizing the scoodr tucked it under his arm and hurried down the street till he reached Eddie's cottage. He had for some reason in his pocket a Christmassy label, salvaged from the neck of an unsaleable because broken doll in the store, bearing the legend "With love from Santa!" This he affixed to the handle of the scooter and because he could hardly drop it down the chimney, leaned it against the wall next to the front door, and went on his way rejoicing.

Frosty though next morning was, an ecstatic Eddie was to be seen testing his scooter skills on the sidewalks outside his house, and when James emerged from his, wobbling on a new bicycle he had not yet learnt to ride, Eddie swept triumphantly past him. Then James remembered a former toy he could ride, and hunted for it in vain. Soon he complained to his father, who in due course confronted Eddie's father, who was as surprised as his son was delighted at the gift he had received. A dreadful moment ensued when James was able to point out faint markings in the paintwork where he had crudely scratched his name.

"It's mine!" James cried. "You stole it!"

"Santa gave it to me," Eddie insisted, clinging on to his prize.

"Someone left it at our door. We didn't ask for charity!" frowned Eddie's father defensively.

"Evidently the boy, or *somebody*," replied James's father with an accusing glance at Eddie's, "purloined it. It will have to be returned, I'm afraid, and no more will be said. Otherwise—"

"Certainly it will be returned," said Eddie's father acidly. "Come on, Eddie, let go of that old thing. Santa would never have given you anything so obviously second-hand!"

Reluctantly Eddie let it go, and went home beside his father, Eddie crestfallen, his father indignant, with his proud head held high.

Christmas celebrations continued. James's father toasted the season in Fleur du Cap, Eddie's in root beer. James hurt his leg in yet another fall off his bike. His twoyill scoodr again occupied its neglected position in the middle of his parents' sweeping lawn. Eddie disconsolately bounced a plastic ball on the patch of ground between his cottage and the road. Tweetie in vacant rather than pensive mood absent-mindedly sucked a lollipop. Belinda, her maternal instincts awakened by a Nativity tableau at the local church, solicitously put a pretty doll to sleep in a little doll's bed under a pink coverlet. Nick pondered the intricacies of the differential calculus, and wondered whether there were any moral lessons he should be drawing from the apparently insoluble problems it posed.

28

A Conundrum

"A logical mind, my dear Watson," Sherlock Holmes said, wreathing a halo of tobacco smoke about his undeceivable head, "must pursue a clue to its unavoidable conclusion even though political expediency should make it impossible for justice to be done."

"Barbaric!" cried Watson.

"Here, for example," said Holmes, blowing another halo, "is such a clue." He held up a torn sheet of good paper, on which was inscribed, under what appeared to be a bloodstain, the mysterious legend "H. 4.1.34."

"Blood, certainly," said Dr Watson, examining the paper. "Do you suspect—*murder*?"

"You are perceptive, Watson. 'Murder most foul, as in the best it is!' But murder where and by whom? Whoever sent this clue to me did not trouble, or manage, to conceal the fact that this paper once bore a parliamentary letterhead. It came, therefore, from the upper echelons of society. We suspect a political motive."

"Fingerprints?"

"Really, Watson! Naturally I was careful not to leave my own before testing the paper, and its envelope, for prints. The paper bore none, the envelope only those of the postman."

"Are you suggesting the *postman* was the culprit?"

"Intuitive guesswork, Watson," said Holmes scathingly, "may be of use in medical diagnoses, but not in detective work." This time he practically disappeared behind the cloud of smoke from his pipe. "Because a rival of mine, Father Brown, has claimed that the postman, being so familiar as not to be noticed, may be the guilty party,* you are too ready to jump to a possibly false conclusion."

Suitably chastened, Watson asked, "What are we to make of the message?"

"Ah, that is where the case becomes interesting! What do those figures convey to you?"

"Very little," Dr Watson admitted. "A grid reference?" When the detective's lips curled contemptuously before closing firmly on his pipe, Watson defensively suggested, "To somewhere beginning with H: Hounslow, Harwich, Hungary—"

"Hardly! Whoever taunted me with this clue would have been more specific than that. It's a literary reference, Watson, to the Act, Scene and line of the most famous play that begins with H—one that I have already quoted in this conversation!"

---

* See G.K. Chesterton's detective story "The Invisible Man" in *The Innocence of Father Brown*.

"*Hamlet!*" cried Watson, as if he had solved the puzzle himself. "But what does the line say?"

"To save you the trouble of looking it up, my dear Watson, I will tell you that it reads 'Hamlet in madness hath Polonius slain.' Now what do you understand by that?"

"That mad Hamlet killed Polonius."

"You say that because you know the story. You are not thinking grammatically, Watson. The line is ambiguous. At that point in the play Rosencrantz and Guildenstern, to whom it was addressed, could not have known whether it meant that mad Hamlet had killed Polonius, or that Polonius had killed mad Hamlet. Or indeed that mad Polonius had killed Hamlet. We are left wondering whose was the corpse and whose the dementia."

"Perhaps Hamlet killed mad Polonius," Watson suggested with a laugh. "I rather think he deserved it!"

"That, English grammar will not allow, Watson. The phrase 'in madness' is too far from the object of the verb. Let us turn our attention to modern times, and ask who may have committed the crime he boasts of so enigmatically, and who his unfortunate victim was."

"That is surely insoluble."

"Oh, far from it. We know that Hamlet was a Prince, and Polonius a Prime Minister. We know that the note came from Parliament. We have only to find, in recent times, a Prince and a Prime Minister, one of whom was mad and one of whom died in what may prove to have been undisclosed circumstances."

"You are too subtle, Holmes."

"Just logical, with an eye for recent history. And we mustn't forget Ophelia, who hoped to marry Prince Hamlet, till she realized, or imagined, he was mad. Now Princess Mary of Teck was groomed to marry the son and heir of the future Edward VII and Queen Alexandra, but when Prince Albert

Victor proved to be, shall we say, unbalanced, so unbalanced that the Ripper murders were at one time ascribed to him, the politicians realized something had to be done. The Prince conveniently died, and the Princess married his brother, subsequently George V."

"Do you mean that the murderer, or his accuser, wants you to read the cryptic line as saying *Prime Minister Polonius killed mad Prince Hamlet?*" Watson asked, wide-eyed.

"That seems to be the logical conclusion in this case."

"Who was Prime Minister when Prince Albert died? Gladstone? Salisbury? Do you mean to say one of *them murdered* him? Preposterous, Holmes!"

"Not impossible, but improbable, Watson! Nevertheless I consider the case solved, but not closed."

"What do you mean?"

"Why, have you not seen the flaw in our reasoning?"

"*Our* reasoning? I have no notion that I was involved in any reasoning."

"Is it not absurd to think *they* would have sent me a confession? Or what could be the motive behind so obscure an accusation, with no hope of a conviction, or seeing justice done? No, it was a hoax meant to test my powers of deduction!"

"Despicable, Holmes! Who could be responsible for such a trick?"

"Why, who was it brought the envelope containing the paper?"

"The postman?"

"After all, Watson, we are brought back by the evidence to none other than the invisible postman!"

"Amazing, Holmes! Then my intuition was right."

"Not entirely. We have yet to ask, Who was the postman?"

"I suppose we could enquire at the post office, if you really want to know."

"Unnecessary. The letter was brought to me on a salver, by you yourself, Watson. Need we look any farther for the postman, and if the postman, surely also the writer?"

"Astounding, Holmes! Simply astounding!"

"No, Watson. Elementary!"

He blew so thick a cloud that Watson was forced to retire, coughing.

29

At the End of the Rainbow

duos habet colores, coeruleum, qui est aqueus, et rubeum, qui est igneus... quadraginta annis ante judicium non videbitur arcus.

The rainbow has two colours, blue, like water, and red, like fire... for forty years before the Judgement the bow will not be visible.

(Petrus Comestor, 12th century)

"**M**ummy, what's a rainbow?" little Jenny asked, her face puckered as she peered out of the window.

"A colourful bow in the clouds when it rains," her mother answered.

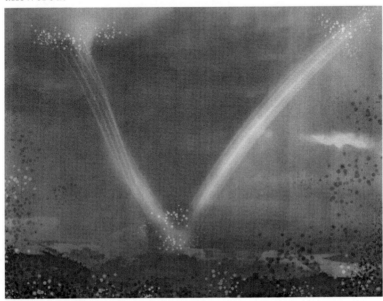

"It's raining now."

"I can't see one at the moment, but it'll be somewhere. Mind you," her mother added thoughtfully, "I can't remember when I last saw one!"

"I've been saying for some time," said a worried physicist, "that refraction is no longer occurring in the clouds! No one will believe me, because you can still see the colours of the spectrum through a prism or when shining a light through spray from a hosepipe, but one day people will have to admit that rainbows have simply disappeared from the sky!"

Eventually the media heard the rumour and publicized what scientists were still saying was impossible. Headlines appeared, facetious, alarmist or thought-provoking, such as "Bows bow out," "Was Newton's explanation wrong?" "Are drugs making us colourblind?" People wrote in claiming either never to have seen a rainbow, or not since childhood. No one asserted they were still commonplace. Theories were offered, most of them too sceptical, ridiculous or fanciful to be worth recording, but the most incredible one of all caught the imagination of doom mongerers and soon swept consternation into the hearts of the susceptible the world over.

According to an ancient legend, rainbows would cease forty years before doomsday. No one could say when the last one had been observed, but the general consensus was that it must have been many years ago. Scholars began hunting for versions of the legend in early texts, and a theologian explained that the blue colour in the rainbow represented the destruction by water that had occurred during Noah's Flood, happily past and non-recurrent, and the red the fire that would eventually destroy the world. Scientists had long known that the planet could not last for ever, but till now popular belief had regarded the inevitable as indefinitely postponed.

If the end of the world was coming, what, people asked, might bring it about? Once the answer would have been nuclear war; more recently it had become fashionable to expect an asteroid strike. Perhaps, some suggested, the energy from a supernova, a star that had exploded some million or so years ago, might reach us at last with obliterating force; alternatively the suction of the black hole supposed to be absorbing material at the centre of the Milky Way might swallow us like the last gurgle of bath water swirling away down the plug hole.

"No, global destruction has to be by fire," adherents of the old legend insisted.

Then seismic readings began to detect abnormal activity under the centre of the United States. In Yellowstone park the geysers bubbled more spectacularly than usual. Old Faithful spurted to twice its usual height and began to rain scalding water on to the viewing platform of the nearby lodge.

"There is a far larger concentration of explosive material waiting to burst forth than we ever imagined," an excitable vulcanologist unwisely informed a journalist, and soon the news echoed round the world that the Americas were in danger of being split apart, with flaming rocks dropping like incendiary bombs as far afield as Hawaii, Scotland and Spain; then a dust cloud blotting out the sun would plunge the entire planet into a freezing darkness that would persist for years, putting an end to photosynthesis, to plant life, to animals and to whatever vestiges of humanity might have escaped the original holocaust.

"Fish may survive, where the sea hasn't boiled," someone suggested cheerfully, "starting the whole process of evolution over again. Who knows what wonderful creatures a million or so years may produce this time?"

"Who cares?" someone else replied.

"It's like a disaster movie!" someone claimed.

"Generally in those a clever young adult in the middle of a romantic attachment, usually female and unfairly

118

disadvantaged, manages to find the only way to save the world," someone else observed hopefully.

"I wonder what the solution will be this time?"

No one except the gloomiest pessimists had any doubt that there would be a solution.

It was a bow in the clouds, projected by a teenager's electronic gadget, the latest rival-crunching product in the ongoing economic warfare of computer technology.

"Look, Jenny," said her mother, "a rainbow! Can you see the colours?"

Whether she could or not, the worried physicist did. "Violet, indigo, blue, green, perhaps yellow," he counted, "but that's all!"

Newspapers appeared with front page headlines: "Redless rainbows sighted." A riddle went viral: "Why is a rainbow like a University textbook?" The answer was: "Neither is re(a)d!"

"We need no longer fear the judgement by fire," the theologian confidently asserted.

As more rainbows were sighted, flashed by competitors the world over, the physicist became more worried than ever. "They exhibit a pronounced shift towards the blue end of the spectrum," he observed.

"Each is bluer than the last," ordinary persons told one another.

"What does blue signify?" people asked, laughing.

"As in the days of Noah—" the theologian quoted darkly.

In Yellowstone the geysers were subsiding to a tourist-disappointing trickle, as the subterranean forces that energized them rippled westwards, where they gathered to a greatness, seeking a vent under the sea. In the middle of the Pacific a huge water spout rose skywards, and a tremendous surge thrust compasswide, gathering intensity rather than exhausting itself as it sped towards land, engulfing island after island on its unstoppable way.

30

The Cuckoo in the Lighthouse

"… the Cuckoo-bird,
Breaking the silence of the seas
Among the farthest Hebrides."
(Wordsworth)

That silence was broken for the lighthouse-keeper and his family by the wind howling down the valley, stirring up the incoming tide to foaming white water that swirled against the rock on which the lighthouse stood. As dark clouds lowered, a damp drizzle intensified till lashing rain sang against the windows in the tower and hissed and bubbled as it steamed

away from the hot cover of the revolving light at the top of the ancient building.

"Can we get home in time?" asked the wife anxiously. "The tide is already beginning to cover the causeway."

The lighthouse keeper gunned the engine, and the tall tyres of his fourwheel-drive slushed through the incoming wavelets breaking over the pathway that was only negotiable for a couple of hours every day. The headlights flashed on the reflecting glass on top of the marker sticks between which he had to drive.

"Step on it, Dad," squealed Jeremy.

"I'm frightened," Kate whimpered.

"We'll be in time," grunted their father, gritting his teeth, and "stepping on" the accelerator. But the waves were getting higher; one larger than usual splashed against the side of the vehicle, spraying the occupants as they clung nervously to the straps next to the doors.

But they gained the ledge in front of the lighthouse, tumbled out, bent over against the rain, and hurried indoors as fast as they could. They hung wet outer garments on hooks against the ground floor walls, and climbed the stairs that spiralled round the inside of the building to the bedroom below the room containing the revolving lamp. It did not take the children long to fall asleep once they were put to bed, despite the thunderous peals that "crashed across the heavens," and "the jagged streak of the levin bolt" that fitfully flashed through the lighthouse windows. The roaring wind whipped up abnormally high waves that tested the walls of the ancient structure, and the keeper's wife looked anxiously out as the deepening tide rocked their transport on its ledge outside the door.

"It's moving! It's gone!" she cried, as a surge larger than they had ever seen there before lifted it clear of the ground and hurled it into the sea. At almost the same time a yacht scudding into its place wedged for a fearful wrecking moment against the rock, and a flash of lightning showed a dark figure hurled from the slanting deck almost against the door of the lighthouse.

As the keeper raced down the stairs, his wife, frozen with horror, found herself unable to cry out to him not to open the door. The smashed yacht had already been swept away and the next huge wave was rearing backwards preparatory to crashing down on the very walls of the building. Torn from the keeper's grasp the door swung outwards and as the sea descended he grasped under the armpits the prone figure that lay just near enough to be reached. The next moment the pressure of the wave slammed the door shut as, knee deep in swirling water, he dragged the unconscious sailor inside.

It was a woman, enveloped in waterproofs. Hauling her on to a nearby settle and vigorously pumping the abdominal muscles so that jets of water spurted from her mouth, the keeper managed to restore first a pulse, then breathing, and finally consciousness.

Her husband, it appeared, had been washed off the yacht and lost in the storm; she had clung to the mast, been hurled dizzily around, and could tell them no more, except that her name was Perdita.

Next day the sea was as unruly as ever, though the weather had lightened, but there was no means of getting off the rock. Provisions soon ran low, and eventually it became imperative that since there was no sign of a rescue mission from the mainland, somehow a message had to be sent along the still submerged causeway. Waiting till the tide was at its lowest, the keeper prepared to make his desperate bid to gain the shore before the sea closed in again and overwhelmed him.

"Keep the children away from me," growled Perdita; "I cannot bear their hungry eyes!"

They would have been less hungry, their mother thought, had they not had a visitor to rescue from the storm. But she could think of little but her husband's safety as he tried to negotiate the dangerous passage to the mainland on foot, wading, swimming, battling the currents.

Perdita, grimacing grimly, smugly observed, "Now we have both lost a husband!"

"Mama, look!" little Kate cried. The door, pummeled by the sea, was loose on its hinges, swinging to and fro in the rising wind.

"Help me shut it," Perdita directed, the mother and her children following her down the staircase.

The door swung outwards. "Quick, catch it!" Perdita ordered, and Jeremy tried to do so. Next moment he was sprawling on the rock, desperately trying to get a handhold. His mother rushed to his aid, wind and water striving to take her legs from under her, and found both children clutching her hands. As she turned she heard the door bolt strike into its socket.

"Open, open!" they screamed, pounding their fists against the door, but there was no answering word, only a face at an upper window that soon withdrew.

The tide was not yet in. Delay meant certain death; but unless rescue came they could not hope to reach the mainland.

"Come children," called their mother, "Perdita will not let us in, but your father is coming and we must splash through the sea as fast as we can to meet him!"

Dragging them after her she began to run along the causeway. Behind them there was a tremendous crash as lightning struck the roof of the lighthouse and a fierce blast of wind caused the whole sea-weakened structure to collapse inwards upon itself.

Lightning Source UK Ltd.
Milton Keynes UK
UKOW02f0141110516

274010UK00001B/46/P